FOREVER IS A REALLY LONG TIME

The Truth About Sex and STDs

By Kelly S. Bolton

ISBN (Print): 978-1-54399-361-5
ISBN (eBook): 978-1-54399-362-2

A very creative way to get information out to both women and men about the impacts of sexual activity…not just about the "birds and bees." Loved the way you tackled the impact of your old field (HSV and Valtrex) and how it can impact people's lives now and also in the future. Great bringing in the other impacts of sex and other diseases and even unwanted pregnancy.

I loved the stories that you made and have heard and experienced very similar stories with my patients. Very interesting with the male writers. It also gave me insight of what the patients may be thinking after the doctor's visit. I think it will hit home with many readers…make them think about it. In addition…very thoughtful about how society has changed its view on sex.

We probably all need a Dr. Thompson Book in our lobby.

—Andrew N Sun, MD/FACOG, OB/GYN

To my husband and kids for their love and support

CONTENTS

Kelly: Insider Information.................................1

The Quiz.................................6

Sonia: One Mistake.................................10

Tanya: "DINK".................................18

McKenzie: "Pick One, Please".................................25

Courtney: *Only* 4000.................................34

Rebecca: They Brought Me Flowers.................................41

Joe: Listen to Me!!!!!.................................46

Lissa: Mended.................................53

Tori: Why Not Me?.................................56

Veronica: Boxer Shorts Condoms?.................................62

Ryan: My Turn.................................69

Jordan: Playing with Fire.................................72

Madelyn: Not Me!!.................................78

Julianna: Super G.................................83

Dr. Melanie Thompson: Cleared for Take Off.................................89

In Case You Missed It.................................92

Addendum.................................96

Works Cited.................................99

Kelly: Insider Information

When the question of "Mom, when can I get a cell phone?" arose at the age of ten, I told my son that I didn't get my first cell phone until I was twenty-six. He was curious as to why I couldn't get my hands on one until I had already become a grown up, and I reminded him that it was because cell phones hadn't even been invented when I was his age. Of course, he was in awe of how old I was, marveling at my existence as if I were one of those prehistoric dinosaurs he'd learned about in school. A brief moment like this reminded me of just how different our current youths' world is compared to the one that I grew up in. Today, my children are exposed, overexposed, and bombarded with more media and information than I could ever imagine. Their smartphones and school-issued laptops provide them with 24/7 access to the Internet, and thus, whatever lies on there also lies at their fingertips. As a result, the modern generation is more likely to explore their sexuality online before they do in person. The chances of a child stumbling upon a Sex Ed campaign during one of these "explorations": slim to none.

By now, we're all aware that change is an inevitable byproduct of time, but how exactly do we adapt as parents? When my parents had "the talk" with me, it lasted all of about ten seconds. In a nutshell I was told that sex before marriage was forbidden, unforgiveable, and simply not an option. Additionally, I was told that no man would ever dare to marry a non-virgin. I listened. I believed. It was most certainly a different time.

I knew that reusing the same "talk" I was given would never be enough to satisfy my children's appetite for information or their curiosity. After all, they've grown up in an era where an overabundance of information is presented to them instantaneously. So I decided to gather some of the moms in my circle, and together, we began discussing the best approach to tackling the subject of sex: what information to share, how much to tell them, and what our kids really need to know.

As we started to narrow down what we would discuss with our kids, most of the moms were surprised, even shocked, at my suggestions. They weren't shocked at my bluntness (I'm a Jersey girl born and bred) or because it was too much for them to handle, but rather because they themselves weren't aware of the facts, the statistics, and the information that I was sharing.

The main message I wanted to deliver to my kids was that **safe sex is a myth**. For me, this is the crucial piece that I believe too many of our teens are uninformed about. I strongly believe that my children, that all children, should be aware of ALL of the risks of diseases that last a lifetime, diseases that kill, diseases that cause cancer, diseases that are widespread and prevalent, diseases that cause infertility, and diseases that can be **transmitted even while using a condom**. Everyone's reaction when I expressed my message was:

1. How do you know all that?
2. How come I don't know that?
3. Can you talk to my son/daughter?

I've spent over 26 years of my career in the healthcare industry working with doctors and nurses, particularly those who treat sexually transmitted diseases (STDs). I'm not a clinician, but I have witnessed and experienced a lot during my tenure. At the time, I had no idea that the information I had access to was largely unknown to people outside of my field. One of my friends once jokingly told me that it was as if I had "insider information" that only doctors have. Actually the information I know is no secret; still, unfortunately, many people find out this "insider information" **after** it's too late. They find out after a trip to their doctor the grim statistics on how common HPV is or that herpes lasts a lifetime. Of course kids and teens need to be educated on a lot more than just the negative aspects of having sex, but it appears that they don't know enough about the dreadful ramifications that **can** and **do** affect sexually active people every single day.

I know that most teens today are free to do what they choose to, and we can never expect to control them. The objective of this book rather is to make sure they have all the facts before they make their decision when to have sex. **We must ensure that our teens make an educated decision**. Isn't that what we're supposed to do as adults—gather information and then make an informed decision? Our youth today are smarter and more savvy than my generation was in several ways. However, many are making risky choices without knowing exactly and entirely what the outcome can be, and for many will be. It is unfathomable to me that the generation being brought up in the information age is still clueless to the facts of life. If they knew what I knew, what countless doctors have witnessed, what the thousands of teens who have contracted an STD experienced and lived through, many will make different decisions.

While doing my own research on "talking to your kids about sex," I was surprised to learn two themes were common and repeated in the books and literature. The first echoed theme is the debate regarding what is the appropriate age to start talking to your kids about sex, and second, how important it is to refer to the body parts by their correct anatomical names. Parents know that all kids differ tremendously in terms of their levels of growth and maturity. I don't believe age is particularly significant unless it's too late. There is no perfect age to start the conversation. I initiated the conversation with my own children at different ages because they matured at different times. Additionally, at least for my family, there seems to be no compelling reason for using only anatomically correct words. If that is stopping you from having a discussion because it's awkward then use whatever words you want to. Who cares which words you choose; just get your point across.

I do believe, however, that it is **much more important** to know what can and does happen **every day** to people who have sex, even with one exclusive partner while using protection, in a very specific context. Kids know that they can get STDs but are they aware that some of these diseases never go away, cause cancer, cause infertility, are spread through oral sex? Do their parents know?

As I mentioned previously, there is an overflow of information today that is available at our fingertips; still too many people do not realize how dangerous sex can actually be. When I searched my local bookstore for advice on discussing sex with my kids, I stumbled upon a 150+ page teen handbook on sex. It contained three full pages, including illustrations, on how to correctly put on a condom and one page citing extremely general information about STDs. I believe most teens can figure out how to use a condom without too much trouble. But I am not confident that these same teens are capable of listing which STDs **CAN** still be transmitted even with a properly applied condom.

The bottom line, in my experience, is that the American population doesn't know enough. If you'd like to test your knowledge on the subject of sex, feel free to take the 14-question quiz below. Many parents struggle to discuss sex with their kids and end up muddling through it, or worse saying nothing. What I want parents to realize is that there is no one-size-fits-all to discussing sex with your children. However, there is one absolute mistake: not starting **and continuing** to have these important conversations.

Just like our kids, parents are unique and have different levels of comfort when discussing sex with their kids. Most of us are probably not comfortable discussing the nuts and bolts of the topic, not to mention the emotional issues that come along with it. I hope that when teenagers and even adults read the stories that follow, they will be better equipped to make informed, educated decisions. My hope (and reason for writing this book) is that it will start a dialog, and maybe some young people will delay the decision to have sex once they have all the data they need, they require, and they **deserve** to make the choices that will affect them possibly for their **entire** lives.

Repeatedly throughout my workday, doctors would tell me about yet another young woman who was diagnosed with a life-altering STD. Of course no names were ever given, just another story of another patient leaving the office in tears. Unfortunately, most of the young women or even girls came to see the doctor after their exposure. It was frustrating for the doctors who wished they had an opportunity to speak to these girls **before** they had sex. I too found myself itching to tell every woman about these stories **before** they embarked on their sexual journeys, not after.

So that's what I did. I wrote these stories based on over two decades of hearing about the realities of sex from doctors, nurses, and even my own friends. The characters are fictional, including Dr. Thompson, but based on real anecdotes I heard repeatedly about real patients, real people. Dr. Thompson is an OB/GYN who asks her patients to write their stories in a journal she keeps in her waiting room in hopes of educating her patients on the dangers of teenagers having sex. I hope and pray this book finds every young woman, teenager, divorced mom, and parent who has yet to learn the entire truth about the consequences of sex. I hope this book finds you before you need to know, not after. I hope you pass the book on to another young person you know. I hope one day everyone knows what I know.

The Quiz

(There may be more than one correct answer to the questions.)

1. Which sexually transmitted disease can be transmitted through skin-on-skin contact vs. through bodily fluids? (This means that condoms will not always protect you.)

    a. Herpes Type 1 and 2
    b. Human Papilloma Virus (HPV)
    c. Hepatitis C
    d. HIV

2. Which STD can cause infertility in women?

    a. Chlamydia
    b. Herpes Type 2
    c. Herpes Type I
    d. Hepatitis C

3. What percentage of women will contact Human Papilloma Virus (HPV) within their lifetime?

    a. 40%
    b. 60%
    c. 80%

4. Which STD(s) last for a lifetime?

    a. Hepatitis A

    b. Herpes Type 2

    c. Hepatitis B

    d. HIV

5. Which STDs can be life-threatening?

    a. Hepatitis B

    b. Syphilis

    c. HPV

    d. Chlamydia

    e. Candidiasis

    f. Herpes Type 2

    g. HIV

6. True or False? If someone has genital herpes but they are not currently having an outbreak (no signs or symptoms), they can pass genital herpes on to their partner.

7. What is the most common STD?

    a. Gonorrhea

    b. Syphilis

    c. HPV

    d. Herpes Type 2

8. Which STDs can cause liver damage?

9. Untreated _____ can cause heart damage, brain damage, spinal damage, psychosis, and blindness.

10. Which STD(s) can be passed on to an infant during delivery?

    a. Gonorrhea

    b. HIV

    c. Herpes Type 2

    d. Chlamydia

11. _____ and _____ can cause infertility in men.

12. Condoms and oral contraception are reported to be 98 to 99% effective in preventing pregnancy, meaning

    a. 1 in 100 statistically will get pregnant

    b. 1 in 1000

    c. 1 in 10,000

    d. 1 in 100,000

13. Which STD can cause hair loss, joint pain, vision problems, and arthritis?

    a. HPV

    b. HIV

    c. Disseminated candidiasis

    d. Gonorrhea

14. What STD has been linked to throat cancer?

    a. Syphilis

    b. HPV

    c. Chlamydia

    d. Herpes Type 1

How Did You Do?

Answer Key

1. a and b

2. a

3. c

4. a, b, c, and d

5. a, b, c, d, e, f, and g

6. True

7. c

8. b and c

9. Syphilis

10. a, b, c, and d

11. Chlamydia and gonorrhea

12. a

13. c

14. b

Sonia: One Mistake

Dr. Jill, my therapist, tells me that I'm "making progress." I don't believe her. I don't see an end to this nightmare, this one mistake I made eight years ago. I can't seem to move forward with my life. I had sex with a guy eight years ago and my life hasn't been the same since then.

I have a date with a really nice guy, Rob, that I met at the gym this Saturday night and I can already tell you today, 4 days out, exactly how this will go. I'm no psychic but history most definitely repeats itself. My dating life has been a replay of the same messed up scene over and over again for several years now. Saturday night will end exactly how all my other date nights have. Nothing seems to change. How is that progress?

Dr. Thompson, my OB/GYN, asked me to write my saga in her waiting room book. Dr. Jill thought it might be therapeutic for me. You see, Dr. T has this journal which is basically chapter after chapter of several of her patients' experiences which lead them to her. She keeps the mostly hand-written journal, really just loose-leaf paper, in a three-ring binder in her waiting room and new chapters continue to get added every time another patient walks in with a bad experience who is willing to share her story. There was a blank cover page but someone handwrote, "I Wish I Knew." Not a bad title.

Every time I have an appointment at the OB/GYN office, sadly, more chapters appear. Each chapter of the book tells a different yet similar story of girls like me who made a mistake, a bad decision, and desperately wish we could go back in time, you know hit the reset button. Each girl in the book agrees to share her experience anonymously and writes another sad chapter to the book. The journal is Dr. T's attempt to educate more women about what can happen hopefully before they decide to have sex or at least before they get a disease. She asked me to contribute my story and have it shared with her other patients so that they'd know what could end up happening to them. She reminds me of the hundreds of young women just like me who she has diagnosed with an STD at a young age and how they repeatedly say to her, "**I wish I knew** before I had sex that I could get an STD even with a condom," or "I wish I knew I could get cancer from sex," or "I wish I knew I could get an STD from oral sex." Dr. T often gets frustrated because so much of what she encounters is PREVENTABLE! I wish I had read that book before I had sex. There definitely would have been one less chapter.

I've now read Dr. T's waiting room journal in full and can relate to the anguish, sadness, embarrassment, pain, and despair that these women have suffered through in their stories. Now my story will be read along with the other tales from my doctor's unfortunate patients. I just wish I'd actually read that journal sooner instead of just scanning the titles and setting it down on the coffee table once again. Maybe it would've stopped me from having sex that night. I believe it would have.

Writing out my story has had a larger impact on my psychological health than my actual therapy sessions. Maybe my therapist was right about that; after all, she's the one who strongly encouraged me to write my story. The thought of my personal account saving another young girl from making the same mistake I made somehow feels like it's lightened my burden, maybe even gave me a purpose. Knowing maybe my story prevented another girl from making a similar mistake made it a little easier to write down on paper my very personal tale. So enough stalling, here we go…

I remember all those ridiculous phrases I told myself as a college freshman.

You only live once. (Now it's a word: YOLO.)

You're only young once.

You should enjoy your college years.

These are the best four years of your life.

You'll want to have crazy college stories to tell when you're older.

I reminded myself how hard I worked to get into Penn State. It was my stretch school, not my safety school. I didn't really date much in high school. Most of the boys were immature, and I was purely focused on getting good grades, playing field hockey, and getting into a really good college. Fast forward a couple months, and I'm telling myself that having casual sex is "normal behavior" for a college student and that nobody wants to be a virgin at my age.

My mom told me to at least wait until I was in love or in a committed relationship before having sex. "Your first time should be with someone special," she would say to me as we set the dinner table before Dad came home. I really just wanted to get it over with. I felt like I was the only virgin in college. I know now that's absolutely not true. Being a virgin, a good student, in the choir, and not exactly fitting into the "in" crowd never bothered me in high school but for the first time in my life I just wanted to "fit in" and be like everyone else. I guess I'm a late bloomer. I worked hard to get here; it was time to start enjoying myself. I was seen as the "good girl" in high school but I began feeling more grown up and more like an actual adult once I started living on my own. I set out to improve and revitalize my social life by seeking out new friends and boys thinking that'd make me feel even more mature. I wanted to be a new girl as soon as possible. I thought that being away at school would allow me to be a different person than I was in high school. And POOF! Just like that, I'd be a different Sonia.

When Danny, Noah, and Brandon from the fourth floor asked my roommate, Zoe, and me to go to their party the second week of school we were so excited. I didn't realize it at the time, but that one night, one encounter, one party would alter my life **forever**. I never "hooked up" with a guy before that night, not even close. My friends told me that you'd be a slut if you didn't wait until the third date but honestly I didn't see a big difference between the first date and the third date. That's not necessarily a committed relationship either. I knew most of the guys at school certainly weren't looking for a relationship, so I didn't hesitate to have sex with Danny that night. Danny was really cute and tall; he played hockey. I felt lucky that he wanted to be with me. I had sex with one guy and used a condom and I got genital herpes. ARE YOU KIDDING ME?? I had friends that had a ton of boyfriends and I know some were having sex in high school and yet never contracted a single STD. Well maybe they did and never told me. I had sex with one guy. Why am I the one that got stuck with herpes?

I really should have known better or listened to my mom. I enjoyed the sex but Danny was not special in any other way. He really didn't pay much attention to me after our hookup. I don't know what I was expecting but something more than a wave here or there. It was obvious that it was just sex for him. I thought it could have been the beginning of something. I was very wrong. It was just sex for him. He, of course, never mentioned to me that he had herpes. I would never, ever do that to another human being. He should have told me.

Dr. T recited all the ominous facts that a person with Herpes Simplex Virus Type 2 needs to know. Unfortunately, I didn't hear most of them. I was in a fog once I heard that horrible word: Herpes. To this day I can't even say it out loud without getting slightly nauseous and triggering some anxiety. I can't remember the last time I have even said the word out loud. I just can't. I did, however, hear Dr. T say very clearly that one phrase which literally haunts me eight years later: "You will have this for the rest of your life; there is no cure."

That's why I find myself in therapy on every other Thursday afternoon and that's why I have so much trouble dating. Can you imagine having to have THAT conversation with **every** guy you start getting close to just before the first time? Having to drop this nuclear bomb on them: "Oh by the way, I have genital herpes type 2." It just became too embarrassing, too depressing, too difficult, too humiliating, and way too predictable.

I would love to meet a great guy and be in a meaningful relationship, or just a relationship, but I tend to avoid relationships because I just can't keep repeating that same scene over and over again. Guys don't stick around after I tell them I have herpes. Some of them are cruel enough to end it right then and there; others are more polite and wait a few weeks or sometimes days before they break up with me for some fabricated and unrelated reason.

I've heard herpes referred to as "the gift that keeps on giving" because it never goes away. It's a virus and it will stay in my body (on the bottom of my spine) forever. From time to time, it comes out of hiding and I get these painful sores. Believe it or not that's not even the worst part about having this contagious disease. People with herpes are certainly contagious when they're having an outbreak, when those painful little sores come out a few times a year, but they, we, are also contagious multiple days every month even when there are no sores, no burning sensation, no itching, basically no signs of an outbreak. This evil little trick is called asymptomatic shedding. So, even if I have no signs of an outbreak, I may be contagious. Please try explaining that to your boyfriend. You can imagine the **hell** I have been through since the second week of my freshman year of college.

Ok, so let's pretend I meet a really great guy who is crazy and about me, is ok with my condition, and even goes as far as to tell me he'll wear a condom every time—no problem, RIGHT? No, not right—it **STILL** gets worse. Dr. T told me that herpes is actually spread through skin-on-skin contact, so my partner may still get infected just by rubbing up against skin that's not protected underneath the condom. She warned me that people with genital herpes are contagious in the **genital region** so my hypothetical boyfriend would still be at risk. A condom **does** help to reduce the disease being spread from one person to another, but it will not work if the infected area is not literally under the condom. It depends on where in the genital area you are contagious. Fabulous.

Bottom line is you are still safer and better off using a condom but it's by no means foolproof.

I haven't completely given up on the idea of a relationship, marriage, or even children but I'll admit I'm thinking about taking yet another extended hiatus from the dating scene. Oh, speaking of that, let's talk about having babies. Herpes can be spread to an infant during delivery so there's a chance, if I ever do meet Mr. Perfect and get pregnant, I'd have to have a C-section. My therapist, Dr. Jill, told me that taking a break from dating is not such a good idea, so occasionally I'll reluctantly embark on another date. I'm not exactly sure how this is supposed to be a good idea because emotionally I've just about exhausted myself. Dating for me is downright depressing. I realize it's not the worst thing in the world that could have happened to me. I could've contracted HIV or another life-threatening illness. I know that thousands of people in the country have herpes just like me and they still date, get married, and have kids. I just can't see how it will all work out for me. I made ONE MISTAKE and I'm paying a very steep price for that one single night in my life.

Hopefully, some Mark Zuckerberg–type entrepreneur will invent an STD-friendly dating app in the near future because if the other person has herpes then I won't have to worry about giving it to him. Doesn't that sound like fun!!! It feels like I'm serving a life sentence, and technically, I guess I am. I've been told I'm being overly dramatic **but how do you think you would feel**? If I hit it off with my date this weekend, in a few weeks I'll have to bring up the conversation. There's nothing like a little STD talk to cool off the heat of a relationship. It's not worth the hurt or pain, so I'll probably break it off before we ever start to get close to that point. Why start something when I know exactly how it will end? There are thousands of other single, clean, and attractive girls out there. Why wouldn't these guys break up with me and find one of those girls who are disease-free?

Ellen, the nurse in Dr. T's office, tells me that she knows plenty of people in my shoes who date and get married and lead a normal life. I think she's been talking to my therapist. I try to be optimistic but right now, today, it's still difficult. Imagine you had that going on down there, knowing you'll never be the same again. I mean I guess I knew what could happen. I obviously knew people could get STDs from sex; I just never ever thought it would happen **to me, my very first time, even with a condom**. Now that you know, maybe you'll think twice before having casual sex.

Thankfully, I attended a large school and was able to avoid Danny for a very long time. I did have to switch dorms. I practiced in my mind at least thousand times what I would say to him when I eventually run into him. I spent many sleepless nights acting out the encounter in my mind. I really wanted him to not just know but to UNDERSTAND what his callousness did to me. I wanted him to know that I almost dropped out of school. I had a hard time coming back after I went home for the weekend to see Dr. T after getting symptoms. My parents knew something was wrong and were very concerned but I couldn't tell them. They were worried sick about me. I imagined Danny talked to his friends about how easy I was and how stupid I was to have sex with some guy I just met. I was really worried about my reputation. I looked into transferring to other schools. I wanted him to know that I was so depressed I had trouble getting out of bed some days and failed one of my early morning classes. My parents paid all that money and I failed the class because I literally could not get out of bed some mornings. I wanted him to know that that I have been lying to my parents and my friends as to why I have not dated anyone in quite some time. I wanted Danny to know that I spent my 19th birthday in my dorm room crying because I was in the middle of a painful outbreak and feeling hopeless, like I was a diseased and disgusting person. I needed Danny to know that I was on a date and had what my doctor later diagnosed as a panic attack. One minute I was fine and actually enjoying myself, the next my heart started to race and I got extremely warm and sweaty, and then I got tunnel vision. I passed out at a dinner table in a restaurant in front of my date, Chase. It was absolutely humiliating. This panic attack unfortunately was the beginning of several other attacks over the years. I needed Danny to know that I am still not ok.

Eventually I did run into Danny and of course he was walking across campus with another girl. My rehearsed speech did not come to my lips the way I planned but I did angrily tell him, in front of the girl, "I hope you don't believe in karma." I don't exactly remember the rest of my words but it was something like I hope he doesn't spread herpes to any other unsuspecting girl and I hope his sister doesn't get duped by some insensitive, uncaring, selfish prick on her first week away from home. I heard his younger sister, who is in high school, came to visit during the Homecoming weekend. I pray that karma doesn't remember him when he has a daughter who starts dating. I'm normally not a confrontational person but seeing Danny with another potential victim gave me the courage I needed to warn her indirectly and finally, hopefully open his mind to the damage he's doing. I believe that some people really don't think it's a big deal to not be upfront about having an STD but obviously it is. I'm trying really hard to be positive and to put this behind me but it's very, very difficult when the herpes, along with the anxiety now, keeps coming back and coming back, and coming back. As I walked away from Danny and that girl, I really hoped she hadn't slept with him yet. I felt as though I started to heal emotionally, maybe just a little bit. Maybe I saved her from going through my ordeal. Maybe my written words prevented someone from suffering what I'm going through. Ladies, I promise you, no matter how cute or popular he is, no matter how good the sex is, no matter how much you want to fit in or don't want to be a virgin, sometimes it's just not worth it.

Tanya: "DINK"

I learned in English class in college that Latin is a dead language. No country, no culture, no population speaks it. When a language is dead no new words are formed. Some people complain when new slang words like "bling," "bestie," and "twerk" are added to the dictionary, but all it means is that the English language is alive and well. My husband and I were called DINKS at a BBQ last year. I didn't even know what the term meant, whether it was a playful insult or a compliment. Mitch, a friend of ours, used the expression. So when I got home I googled it; DINK stands for "dual income, no kids."

The word, or acronym, more accurately, does not have a negative connotation to it, but certainly it does to me. According to Google, couples living in a DINK household are often the target of marketing efforts for luxury items because they have more disposable income. It's kind of a marketing term for a specific audience.

That backyard BBQ conversation revolved around kids as it typically does with our peers. Most of them have kids by now. The term DINK was expressed with a feeling of envy for Jeff, my husband, and me because we have more free time, more money, and more freedom. My friends were complaining about the expenses that pile up as their children continue to grow. I know that there was no malintent on their part, perhaps just some minor insensitivity. Our friends really love their children, of course; it's part humor and part human nature to complain.

Jeff and I were schooled on the cost of diapers for twins in their first year of life, how much a good babysitter costs, the increasing price of formula, and let's not get started on the cost of daycare. Our friends went on about the challenges of juggling their careers with kids, and learning to live on less money. My deep, unspoken, and sometimes angry thoughts were not the slightest bit sympathetic to their woes. Being unable to have children had made me cold and indifferent to the plight of my friends and peers. To be fair, no one in that perfectly landscaped suburban backyard knew that Jeff and I have spent more than $30,000 hoping for a **CHANCE (which failed)** to have a child of our own. We keep our misery private. No one in the neighborhood knows that we are considering taking a second mortgage on our home to have enough money to try and adopt a child.

I am sad, bitter, overly sensitive, and mostly angry with myself. You see, **I did this** to us, to both of us. Jeff, the other half on my DINK equation, is that guy that you meet and quickly realize that he is too good of a man not to hold on to. We were 25 when we met and I was really enjoying my single life, but I knew what I had with him was special, and I was not willing to let him go. Jeff is supportive, kind, intelligent, hardworking, complimentary, handsome, thoughtful, and dishonest. Yes, you read that correctly. It's not an error; I said "dishonest." He assures me over and over that he doesn't blame me, that it's not my fault. He even told me while I was sobbing one night, "It's no big deal" that I am infertile. How can he not blame me, be disappointed in me, or even get angry with me sometimes, once in a while, even just once? I think he's lying and secretly deep down he resents me **just a little bit**. The problem is that he'll never say that to me; it would crush us both and probably change our relationship forever. But maybe I would feel better if he did. This is the definition of a no-win situation. I am very aware of that.

I wish he would just say he blames me just a little bit. I imagine myself sometimes provoking him, starting a fight, even hitting him to get him angry enough to admit that he blames me. I want him to yell at me, get angry, tell me he is disappointed, explain how upset he is that he will never have his own biological child, finally state the truth: It is my fault that we can't have kids.

It's not that I'm a victim of some hard luck and thus cannot bear children. It is because of my behavior, my actions with another man that we cannot have our own children. I cannot imagine how that makes my husband feel. As for me, that is a very bitter pill to swallow. I unknowingly took that possibility away from us years ago. I will never feel a baby inside of me kick or grow. I will never know what our offspring would look like. I will never get to experience pregnancy and childbirth. I know that to a teenager pregnancy and childbirth are probably not appealing; it wasn't to me at all either as a teen. But that changes as you mature. I want to experience all of it. I want Jeff to feel my big belly, hear his baby's heart beating inside of me, watch his baby move for the first time with the ultrasound. All of that is no longer possible because of a decision I made.

I'm the one who contracted chlamydia after having sex with my boyfriend senior year of high school. I'm the one whose undiagnosed STD lead to **permanent, irreversible** infertility. I learned too late that chlamydia, like many other STDs, often goes undiagnosed for months, which can lead to larger problems down the road, such as infertility. Jeff told me all the right things that I needed to hear: "it could have been me," "I was not a virgin when we met," "I had more sexual partners than you." He's so noble, so kind; it's awful that I put him through this.

See, Chlamydia can cause infertility in men but it is much more likely to cause infertility in women. Of course, I didn't know that when I was having sex in high school. It was my previous sexual encounter, not his, my foolish 17-year-old self, my arrogance (no one could tell me anything at that age) that got me here. I thought I knew it all at 17. I thought I'd end up marrying that guy so it was totally ok if we had sex. If I could go back, I would change everything.

Nick was my second boyfriend. If you had a boyfriend in high school it would automatically increase your social status amongst the students. My first so-called boyfriend did not last more than a few weeks. He really, really wanted to have sex. I said no and resisted all of his advances. I quickly realized that he was just in it for the possibility of sex. I barely knew him but I loved the idea of having a boyfriend. Nick was different. Nick and I had a real relationship and we cared about each other. We talked about the future together and he really was a sweet guy. We were together for over a year. I really did like him a lot and thought he would eventually break up with me if I didn't have sex with him. He persisted for months. I eventually acquiesced. I actually wanted to have sex but I was so worried about getting pregnant and ending up another high school dropout. I thought to myself if I got pregnant in college it wouldn't be as bad, but not in high school. I did, at that time, think we would get married, not anytime soon, but when we were a lot older. I mean really how long did I have to wait. We were together for what I thought was a **very long time**.

My high school romance concluded like so many others; we slowly began to drift apart until we went our separate ways. Our colleges were hundreds of miles apart and there were so many new, different, interesting, and cute guys to meet. Nick still talked about staying together and our future together but we became different people. Still, I will never forget Nick for two reasons: he was my first love, and more importantly, he gave me chlamydia. Unfortunately, chlamydia, like so many other STDs, has some consequences that can be permanent. Take a moment to think about that word "permanent." Something you do today can change the rest of your life **FOREVER**.

I did not even know that I had chlamydia until several months after I got it. Like most people with chlamydia, I had no symptoms at all. A week or so of an antibiotic when I had the disease would have cleared up my infection, I've been told. Untreated chlamydia, **now I know**, can turn into PID, pelvic inflammatory disease, which caused me to eventually become infertile. I can never have kids of my own. If I were born like this, unable to bear children, maybe it would not be so hard to accept. I probably would have thought there was some cosmic reason for my infertility. I have so much guilt and regret because it was from my own actions that I ended up with this condition. The irony is not lost on me that my biggest fear as a 17-year-old having sex in high school was getting pregnant. I was so cautious about not getting pregnant. Now I'd give all my money (and already have) for a chance to have my own baby with my husband, the man I deeply love. I want to tell all the teenagers reading this one thing: teenage love is very different from adult love. True, sometimes teen romance does work out long-term. However, these years are when we really grow and change the most. Often it's just too soon to know.

Having sex caused me to become infertile. Now 14 years later, I almost wish I had gotten pregnant with Nick if I knew that would be my only chance to have my own child. I want a baby with Jeff though, not my silly high school boyfriend. Jeff and I used to talk about what our future child would look like, whether it would look more like Jeff or equally part of both of us. Would the baby turn out kind and sensitive like Jeff or determined and Type A like me? It is so unfair that one decision at such a young age altered my whole life and my family's.

My OB/GYN, Dr. Thompson, finally diagnosed my PID and eventually was the one that had to reveal the news of my infertility to me. I cried in her office for 30 minutes. She told me at another visit about the journal of her patients' stories in her waiting room and asked me to write my own story. She knew my husband and my struggles with not being able to conceive our own children. She didn't have to ask me twice. I was eager to write everything down, to pour my emotions out through the ink of the pen.

She said that many of her patients were hesitant to write a chapter in her book, but I wasn't. I wanted young girls to read my story, my agony and my heartbreak. Maybe some of them, or hopefully even a few more than that, will wait to have sex, or get checked out before their chlamydia or another STD inflicts long-term, irreparable damage. I wish I had waited a little longer. At that time in my life, I waited for what seemed like a more than reasonable time; it seemed like "forever." In retrospect, that time was nothing. I should have waited longer.

I have stayed in touch with many of my friends from both high school and college. None of my friends remain with their high school sweethearts, and only a few of the college romances worked out long-term. I foolishly assumed that my high school relationship would withstand the test of time. I, of course, wish I did not have sex with Nick not just because of the PID, but because I only wanted to be with one guy. I know that sounds so old-fashioned, but I thought we would end up together. That is just not what happens most of the time.

I have obviously spent a lot of time thinking about Nick. I assumed I was his first. I didn't even think to ask him about other sex partners; we were pretty young. I wonder how many partners he had. I saw a pamphlet in Dr. Thompson's office printed by Heritage House '76. It graphs out what your sexual exposure is. For example, if you had 3 partners and your partner had 3 partners, you are exposed to the sexual history of 7 people. **It's just math** and the numbers go up exponentially.

5 partners each = your exposure rises to **31**

8 partners = **255** exposures

9 partners = **511** exposures

16 partners = **65,535** exposures

THINK ABOUT IT!

I have a great man, a great partner, in Jeff. He really loves me and is sticking by my side despite all of this. I don't believe that every man would. I know he wants children as badly as I do and that **really** hurts me. I am not the only one paying the price for my prior sex life; he is too and so are my children…yes, my children. I had two miscarriages. When you find out you are pregnant, you don't think of those babies as fetuses or embryos; they are already your babies. Two souls, two cherished lives to love, to hold, to watch grow up, yet to never be born. No one can imagine how heartbreaking that is.

I have heard that our ability to remember things is tied to our emotions. I will never be able to erase the look on my mother-in-law's face when we broke the news to her that we lost the second baby. I saw tears stream down Jeff's face for the first time that day. I've known that man for over 7 years and have never seen him cry before. In my mind, I have punished my husband, my unborn children, my parents, my in laws, my siblings. **I threw a stone into a lake and the ripple effect seems to be infinite**.

My vision is so clear today but there is no going back. If I could go back I would have waited. I would not have had sex with Nick. If I had a glimpse of the heart-wrenching agony and pain that sex had caused me and so many others I love, I would have never had sex with him. I wish I knew that having sex could make my husband and me childless. Ironic, isn't it? I wish I knew.

McKenzie: "Pick One, Please"

I still remember the way my grandmother used to tune into her favorite television show, *I Love Lucy*, **Wednesdays at 8 PM**. Lucy and her husband were married with a son, but they slept in separate beds because even married couples sleeping in the same bed were viewed as scandalous at that time. My mother grew up watching *The Brady Bunch*. Carol and Mike Brady shared a bed but never shared more than a quick kiss on TV. As for my generation, we grew up watching people on *The Real World* getting naked and having sex in a hot tub the first night they met. Sex has been plastered on TV, books, movies, magazines, all over the Internet, on billboards, pretty much everywhere you can imagine. At times it feels as though you can't escape some sort of sexual innuendo being launched your way no matter where you are, or what you're watching. Our magazine covers feature nude or seminude models, and our mainstream TV shows that dominate the airwaves are overloaded with sex. There is *Jersey Shore*, *Sex Box*, *Girlfriend's Guide to Divorce*, *Sex and the City*, *Dating Naked*, *Full Frontal*, *True Blood*, *Entourage*, *Shameless*, and *Teen Mom*. And let's not forget the massive blockbuster hit *Fifty Shades of Grey* and its sequels. I'm not trying to sound judgmental or prudish; I'm simply amazed at the rapid change that has materialized in such a short period of time.

I've always been curious: Are movies a reflection of our current reality or do people imitate what they see on the big and small screen? I'm in my second year of the cinematography program at NYU. One day I will be a movie producer faced with challenging decisions regarding what I choose to include in my films (hopefully). Will my films be a reflection of what I believe modern societal trends are, or will I be setting a trend of behavior and thought through my films? Time will tell, I suppose.

Many of the producers, who make movies, TV shows, and even commercials, attempt to portray realistic scenarios as much as possible. Doctors and lawyers are even hired by studios to provide feedback to make shows more realistic. This is why viewers today frequently see people having children before marriage, enjoying a single girl's life of sex with multiple partners, and living a completely different lifestyle than our parents and grandparents did. I think it's fantastic and real progress that modern women have the freedom to make their own choices. I am glad that women can have children even if they never intend to get married. I mean I can't even imagine what it would've been like to live in the 1950s or any time before that. That being said, I've noticed a huge omission in the media's attempt to realistically portray modern society. They missed something. Something huge.

I am not commenting on the morality or immorality of the change in our culture. I am, however, trying to make the point that the media today is **not quite telling the full story**. Unfortunately, there are often very significant consequences that come with an increase in our sexual activity. I've spoken about the positives that have emerged through this change in cultural norms, but we cannot ignore the glaring negatives that have surfaced as well. These negatives should be shared and portrayed along with the positives; otherwise, we're simply being presented with an unrealistic, almost utopian view of society. Just like the cop shows hiring real cops to make sure their TV dramas are as accurate as possible, television producers should consider hiring a gynecologist or any one of the female writers in this journal as consultants. The contributing authors of this book would inform them that with this newfound sexual freedom comes problems, diseases, regret, emotional issues, infertility, cancer, or even death. Why do we rarely see the negative consequences of sex in the media today? It seems totally ok to have sex, just not so ok to get stuck with an STD. The two unfortunately aren't mutually exclusive.

Women are openly enjoying their sexual freedom (just watch one episode of *Sex and the City* if you don't believe this to be true), and not having marriage or monogamy as their only option in life. Again, I grew up in this generation, so I understand the shift, and I am not against it. What I can't quite understand is why I was bombarded with this acceptance of sexual freedom without being exposed to what may come along with all this sex—thousands upon thousands of diseases being transmitted daily.

I, along with most of my peers, grew up watching all these TV shows and seeing all these characters having sex without much mention of the accompanying dangers. For whatever reason, there were very few shows or movies, if any, with plotlines that depicted the prevalence of STDs and just how devastating they can be. When's the last time your favorite sitcom star got diagnosed with herpes? Rarely do you see someone having to deal with life-altering infertility due to an STD in a sitcom. I was shocked when I read about the other girls in this book. I've probably sat next to them in Dr. T's waiting room as we awaited the horrible news of our respective diagnosis. Hell, one of my closest friends contracted HPV. They say **most of us will eventually get it too**. I wonder how many sex partners the four ladies on *Sex and the City* had in total? I can only recall one episode in which Charlotte was the unlucky one to get crabs. Now I realize how ridiculously unrealistic that really is.

Here is my *Sex and the City* question of the week.

"If casual sex is so acceptable today, why is it still taboo to talk about the diseases in our favorite TV shows and movies? Shouldn't the diseases be part of the dialog since they are part of the package? If it's ok to have sex with multiple partners then there should be no shame in having a disease and therefore being open about it.

Where are the Hollywood stars openly discussing their genital warts the way they proudly show off their baby bumps when they are not even engaged? Why is it so shameful and embarrassing to have an STD? Our culture promotes sexual freedom, so why do we shy away from the diseases that this very freedom causes? The lack of honesty seems a bit hypocritical and misleading, if you ask me. Teenage pregnancy appears to be less taboo and definitely a part of the mainstream of discussion. Diseases, not so much.

So you probably guessed that I am a patient of Dr. Thompson's too. She asked me to write a chapter not because of my strong opinions or my critique of the media, but rather because of my own personal drama. So reluctantly, I agreed. Here it goes.

My parents did almost everything by the book to raise us right. They taught my siblings and me to work hard in school, to pursue our dreams with passion, and to never give up on ourselves. They constantly instilled the values of respect and kindness for others, and made sure that we main-tained a charitable spirit throughout our youth. We were told to eat healthy, spend money wisely, and never smoke or do drugs. However, when it came to talking to us about sex, I really think they missed the boat.

They never instructed us to refrain from sex until we were married, even though they themselves waited. My parents always assumed they couldn't stop my siblings and me from having sex, especially as the youth in America continued to move toward a looser perspective on sexual activity. I always felt they were only being "realistic" and were ok with whatever we decided as long as we protected ourselves. They never told us to wait at least until we were in a serious relationship with a trustworthy partner. They never said we should hold out until we were married or at least in love, or until it was with someone special—the way they did. They never told us what could possibly happen besides getting pregnant. I remember my mom telling me, more than a few times when, in her words, I was a "girl in trouble" that she was "too young to be a grandmother." It's interesting, now that I look back on that comment, that moment; it was about her, not me or my baby.

Mom, how about saying to me…

"**You** are too young to be a mom."

Or

"My grandson deserves a stable family with a mom and a dad and financial stability like you had."

Or

"Your heart will break when he leaves you and your baby."

Or

"You can get diseases, bad diseases."

Or

"You will have to give up your dream of college if you keep your baby."

Or

"If you have your baby and give him up, the hole in your heart will never go away."

Pick one reason, Mom and Dad. Why couldn't you have picked at least one reason? Maybe if you gave me one reason to wait I would have listened or thought twice about it. Maybe if you told me how disappointed you would be in me I would have stopped myself. Why didn't you warn me or try to stop me? Why were you so quick to give up and assume that **I was "going to do it anyway"**?

Victoria, my BFF, once told me her mom said that she'd **kill her** if she ever messed up her life by getting pregnant. I too needed to hear that. Of course, she would never have literally killed her or even disowned her but Victoria was definitely worried and afraid of the possibilities. She got the point. I needed a voice, like Victoria's mom's, in my head that night while I sat in the parked car behind the grocery store with a boy. There was nothing to give me pause and think about what I was about to do, or even why I was about to do it, and most importantly, why I shouldn't do it.

He meant nothing to me. I barely knew Steve when we hooked up. It was nothing special; I was certainly not in love. Steve was cool, cute, and popular; he played football. Just talking to someone like him in high school immediately made me more popular. Girls who ignored me or criticized my brand of jeans a week before were now engaging me in small talk. I never thought I could or would ever get pregnant; we were so careful.

My grandmother always shared her bits of wisdom with me whenever I was going through a difficult time; "this too shall pass" was one of her favorite phrases. Well now I know that expression applies to the good as well as the bad. I was finally in with the cool crowd and my life was awesome. I don't know if adults understand how life-changing it is to go from invisible to popular in high school. But like my grandmother said—it passed. Actually it grinded to a screeching halt the second I found out I was pregnant. Overnight, my membership in the **cool** crowd was rendered meaningless. I was going to miss the prom, graduation, senior parties, senior cut day, the class trip to New York City, all of it because of some guy who meant nothing to me then, and means even less to me now. Worse than that, I was giving birth to another child under unfavorable circumstances. This child deserved more.

On August 14 when all my remaining friends were packing for college, I was in a hospital room screaming in pain and giving birth to my son. I assumed the painful part was going to be the actual birth, the moment he came ripping out of my body, but it was actually the 7 hours of contractions and labor that was the most excruciating pain I have ever experienced up to that point, and I've had a root canal. It felt like the worst cramps I'd ever had, times 5000, and the pain lasted for hours. After he was born, I was in a lot of pain too. My son was over 8 pounds, 8 pounds 4 ounces to be precise; they always tell you the weight. On top of everything, the one thing I was the most nervous and anxious about ended up happening. I tore down there and had to get five stitches. For a week after my son was born, I had to sit in warm water for 20 minutes on a blowup seat I placed over the toilet seat several times a day to heal. My back began to really hurt from the strain of sitting in that spot, and the stitched area was extremely sensitive. Oh yeah, it hurt like hell to pee as well. Little did I know, the worst pain I was ever going to feel was still yet to come.

I knew I couldn't take care of this baby financially or emotionally. I really had no business being a mom and I knew I probably wouldn't be a good one because I was still a kid myself. Steve was no help at all. He was so disappointing. He got into Brown University and was not going to have that interrupted by a 3-month fling or his own child. I also knew my son deserved a stable family, a mom **and** a dad. There was zero chance my baby would have a father at this point. My parents were not offering to raise another kid and I didn't think it was fair to even ask them. How does that work exactly? I'm off at college, which they are paying for, while they're stuck changing diapers and paying for them too and putting off retirement. I had no choice but to do **the most painful thing a mother ever has to do**—I had to give up my baby.

The thing is when you give birth you **immediately form a bond** with that child. I never felt a connection so deep until he was born. I love my family but this was completely different and **much, much stronger**. I never knew I could love anyone so much before I laid eyes on my baby. It happened the **instant**, the exact moment, I laid eyes on him. The pain of giving him up is easily 1000 times worse than the physical pain of labor and delivery, but I knew it was my opportunity to be a good parent and make the biggest sacrifice for him. I completely understand why women in my situation choose to keep their babies. The bond with your child is so strong that it makes it nearly impossible to make this excruciatingly painful decision, but I had to be selfless, for Jack. I knew I would never ever forget him or the love I have for him. I had to give him a proper name, even if it was just known to me. When I think of him I can't think of "that baby" but of my baby, of my baby Jack. I was not allowed to really name him but in my mind and heart he is Jack. The feeling of overwhelming love for your own child is completely indescribable. I love my son more than anything in the world, and I'd only known him for a second. I cried so hard I was afraid I was going to stop breathing. The pain is palpable.

A few years after I gave birth, I was watching that medical channel on TV about childbirth. Researchers put a probe on women's heads during delivery and were able to look at their brainwaves. They saw an actual change in the women's brain chemistry at the exact moment the baby was born. This revelation was surprising I guess to the doctors but not at all to me. My personal experience confirms this phenomenon. When my son finally popped out after nine months of carrying him around and hours of hard labor, I felt something change in me in that instant. I was overwhelmed by love and a need to protect him at all costs. I will never forget that feeling or that love. I had carried him in my body for nine months, felt him move, talked to him, had him to keep me company 24/7 for months, and felt a bond to him but it paled in comparison to the bond I felt when I saw him for the first time. It's amazing.

Even though someone else is raising him and hugging him and comforting him and providing for him every day, I know I love him more than anyone else can. In that moment, I didn't care about the prom, graduation, college, or a career or my friends or what I was missing. None of it mattered to me. I only cared about him and nothing else. I gave him up because for me, his future was the most important thing.

My life has continued and I did go to college, follow my dreams, and get a job in the field I wanted to. But the **feeling of loss never did pass**. I have a good life and my friends think I am a very happy person. I am! But I feel a tremendous sense of loss every single day. Some people who have had arms or legs amputated still feel pain where their limb once was. I saw this on the medical channel too. This phantom pain is real to the person without the limb even though it doesn't seem possible. I feel pain every day in my heart, in my body. I feel the loss of what I gave up. Sometimes I still wonder if I did the right thing—I know in my head that I did but my heart feels very differently.

It has been years now and the hole in my heart never did go away. I feel like a part of my heart was amputated and is aching for my son to come back into my life. I accept that for me, this feeling will never pass. I guess that even my grandma, with all her years of life experience, can't be right about everything; then again she never had to go through anything remotely close to the absolute hell of giving up her own child. Jack will always be a part of me; we will always share a bond. When I had sex with that boy that night 9 years ago, I couldn't have known that years later I would still be reliving the agony. I constantly pray my son never feels the emptiness of abandonment or the pain of loss because his mother decided to give him up. **That** would kill me.

Courtney: *Only* 4000

They call hospice "comfort care." But when I hear the word hospice I know, we all know, what it really means. There is no hope for me, medically speaking. There is no reason to continue treating my condition with drugs. The drugs are now for one purpose only, to manage my pain. Nothing more can be done to save my life. I am going to die, and sex will be what killed me. Yes, I know that is very shocking and dramatic, but sadly, it is very true. Sex didn't end my life quickly and humanely like a well-placed bullet. It waited patiently, not striking until nineteen years later when I had so much more to lose—a family of my own.

It was so embarrassing when my friends and family, particularly my father and brother, were given the news of what I had contracted. If you assumed I have HIV, you are wrong. **There** are actually other diseases you can contract from sex, which can be just as deadly. It seems like we always associate HIV with death, but we fail to acknowledge the other diseases that lie in wait. My friends had never even worried about HIV because we are straight and have never done IV drugs. I never knew that you could actually die from HPV. But just my luck, HPV, or Human Papilloma Virus, happens to be one of the two most common sexually transmitted diseases. And it just so happens, it can be fatal as well. I have **more than a few friends** who have gotten HPV. **It is very common**.

I have cervical cancer, which is caused by the HPV virus. When you tell people that you have cervical cancer it's not like telling them you have breast cancer. Almost all cervical cancers are caused by HPV, so people are right to assume I contracted the virus from sexual intercourse. There is so much shame and embarrassment in that, even though we are all having sex. I'm dying—I shouldn't care about what others think, I shouldn't care about people knowing that I have an STD, but what can I say? I do! I can't escape it and one of the worst parts about it is that one day, my daughter will be told how her mom died.

I feel like I'm being punished for some reason. It's not like I had a dozen partners who might've given me HPV. I got married at 30 years old; it was unrealistic to think that I was going to wait until my wedding night to have sex. Times have changed; almost nobody waits anymore. My mother got married at 20. If I could go back, if I could Monday morning quarterback, if I knew **what could have happened**, there is no doubt in my mind that I would have done things a lot differently. I definitely would have waited. But in reality, maybe I'm not being punished; maybe I'm just that unlucky.

Thousands of women are diagnosed with HPV every year, but only a small percentage of them get cervical cancer from it. According to my doctor, only 4000 end up dead. **Only 4000**!!! In reality that is a small number, or at least as the medical community sees it, a small percentage of the women who get HPV. About 60,000 people die every year from the flu. But if you are one of those 4000, it's not as insignificant as they make it sound. In my opinion, 4000 American deaths are far too many. Especially when you consider that many of these deaths could have been prevented with a little more insight and education into the risks of sex. There are so many people who are suffering and will suffer in the future due to this disease. Imagine reading another 3999 stories in this book year after year after year, from women like me who are **in their final weeks, days, or hours of life simply because they chose to have sex and just simply didn't have enough information**.

I think about the other 3999. Are they like me? Were they also foolish enough to believe that this could never happen to them because they were not promiscuous? Did they sleep with only one or two guys? Who are they leaving behind—parents, a boyfriend, a husband, grandparents, children? Today there are two vaccines, but not everyone will get vaccinated and the vaccine covers eight of the 14 cancer-causing strains. HPV 18 and HPV 18 cause 70% of cervical cancers. Not all the strains that can cause cancer are covered by the vaccines. Plus, what are the odds that your partner has been vaccinated? Many people, both men and women, never got the vaccine. There are dozens of strains of HPV, some that cause cancer, some that only cause genital warts. It's amazing what you can learn today in an instant on the Internet. Too bad I didn't bother to google HPV back then.

I spend so much time lately thinking about my daughter's life without the presence of her mother for all of those countless milestones. Who will help her pick out her prom dress, her wedding dress? I think about the struggles my husband will have being a single parent to a daughter. I think about why I wasn't informed that this could potentially happen to me. I knew that HIV was deadly. I knew that you could get warts and herpes from sex. I certainly knew that you could get pregnant. But I didn't know that the cancer caused by HPV claimed the lives of over 4000 women in this country every year, or that **the vaccine or condoms used to protect us are not close to 100% effective in preventing HPV.**

I had "Family Life" in the fifth grade, but that is too young to be taught about the realities of sex. I had health class in the tenth grade for one month. For a majority of that month, we learned about HIV. It was the early 1990s and HIV was very scary and a "game changer." I remember witnessing the realities of this new epidemic on the nightly news every evening for weeks, maybe even months. It was being reported that **people could actually** now **die from sex**. But even with all of this newfound awareness and coverage, they failed to mention the other diseases that were also deadly. Did the news reporters and the sex education teachers not know that there are other diseases that can kill? Why were we lead to believe that HIV/AIDS was the only deadly STD? I will never know. I never thought I could get cancer and die from an STD other than HIV, because one ever told us that.

I had two long-term boyfriends before I was with my husband. I never once had sex with either of these two boyfriends without a condom. Yet I, like **thousands** of other women, still contracted HPV. My only fear was getting pregnant. I was worried about how I would not be able to go to college if I got pregnant, and how my parents would freak out if they heard the news. Looking back, I would've traded an unplanned teen pregnancy for cancer without batting an eye. I never once worried about dying. No one told me (not my parents, not my health teacher, not my friends, not the nurse at the clinic) that condoms protect better against a disease like HIV, which is transmitted by bodily fluids, and are less effective against protecting from diseases that are caused by skin-to-skin contact like HPV and genital warts (and herpes too, I found out). No one told me that if my partner had HPV somewhere on his genital area not covered under the condom, the protection provided by the condom would be useless.

I was not going to write about this because it is too painful, but maybe my words will educate and enlighten the next generation of girls. My soon-to-be two-year-old daughter Paige will only remember me through photos, from stories from family and friends, and what I write in this entry. Knowing I am leaving her without a mother is unbearable. It's literal torture. It's impossible to articulate how devastating it is to leave a child behind. I know I am dying but I cannot accept the fact that I am leaving her motherless and I have failed to accept the fact that my death and the deaths of thousands of others was preventable not by a condom or by a vaccine but by **information**. I know that many of my questions about life, death, faith, suffering, and the afterlife will never be answered here on this Earth and that I do accept. But I would like to know why no teen magazine, TV show, movie, teacher, or public health official made it their mission to get this information out to teenagers. I realize that information and knowledge might not save every life, but it certainly would have saved mine.

When I started writing my story, I was thinking about calling it "Only 3000." By the time I was able to get my thoughts on paper for Dr. Thompson, I had to change the title to "Only 4000." More and more teens have gotten vaccinated each year since I got my deadly diagnosis, yet the number of cases of HPV and the number of deaths is still rising. Do teenagers who get the vaccine think they are completely immune? Do they understand that the vaccine does not cover all the cancer-causing strains or all of the wart-producing ones? Do they think condoms will protect them? Perhaps the 4000 deaths of young women still aren't enough for the world to take notice, but this year it will be 4001. Please, please, don't make the same mistake I did.

Without a doubt the single most difficult task I've ever had in my life is saying goodbye to Paige. It took well over 20 attempts to write her a letter. She can't read yet but I had so much to tell her, things I needed her to hear from me, her mom. Night after night I started but had to stop my letter so many times because I cried so hard that the pages were wet from tears; it was hard to focus. I decided that I just had to get through it or else she would never know at least a very few of the things a mom needs to say to her daughter. I'm including a very small part of my letter to her for the readers of this book. While this is only meant for my sweet Paige, I want you, the reader of this book, to read part of my words to Paige because it is my way to BEG you to think about what you are doing and how it can so profoundly, so negatively impact you and the people around you. I beg you, on my knees, please, please don't let another family lose a mom, daughter, wife, or sister, because of a PREVENTABLE STD.

I remember that first diaper of yours that I changed. I remember think-ing to myself that it is an HONOR to change your diaper. Sounds pretty crazy, right? Maybe not so crazy. I read that pregnant and post-partum moms can have some pretty wild mood swings from hormones, at first I thought, wow, what a strange thought, but no, that musing was rational and clear. It is an honor and a privilege that I was the one chosen to be your mom. I was the one lucky enough to be picked by God to rock you to sleep, feed you your first meal, dry your tears, listen to you babble, keep you safe, comfort you, hug you, and kiss you, and yes, even change your diaper. I am so profoundly sad for both of us about how many things we will miss like your first day of school, your first steps, your first words, your first dance, your first dance recital or soccer game, your first time driving a car, your first tooth. I can literally go on for pages and days. I want, more than anything, to be there for you for all your milestones and all your regular days, good and bad. I want desperately to be there for every second of your childhood. I'm so sorry. I daydream about a regular day where we are in the car driving home from softball practice and we are singing out loud a goofy 80s song and just laughing. It's a regular day but a perfect day because we are sharing a laugh. I want to give you advice about jobs, money, boys, especially boys, and staying safe, everything. I am so sorry, so very sorry. I want you to know I am with you, watching you, cheering you on with every step of your day, your life, supporting you. I want you to surround yourself with positive experiences, good people, and love and faith.

If I were here, I would show you how to make lasagna. I'm sure you heard I never could cook but I did have one good meal I could make. Everyone should be able to make at least one great dish. I stare at you when you are sleeping; you are an angel from heaven. You are so beautiful I can't even believe I could make anything so perfect. I love you. Please know you are loved, and special, and precious, and amazing.

I tried and failed to put a lifetime of love, friendship, and advice into written words. Unfortunately, it just can't really be done. I pray that you will one day enjoy the blessings of being a mom. Only then will you comprehend the love I have for you. I don't believe there are words or phrases that can begin to describe the depth of the love I have for you. Know that my love for you is greater than the universe and that I am watching you from afar and am always here to listen.

Rebecca: They Brought Me Flowers

I t was a Tuesday in April. I remember it was still very cold and I kept wondering why it wasn't warmer by now. Every spring I'm disappointed that the weather does not heat up on the day I flip the calendar from March to April. That Tuesday was gloomy, cold, and gray—very fitting weather for what was about to happen.

The staff at the clinic was very nice and friendly when I arrived. I remember thinking that they must have taken a course on customer service similar to the one I had to take at work. My office just had us take a class called "Knock Your Socks Off Service." The staff at the clinic really went out of their way to be friendly, polite, courteous, and to have giant, sincere-looking smiles at all times. Hours later when I was being wheeled out of the front door, one of the nurses handed me a small bouquet of flowers as I was pushed out into the miserable, misty, cold street. That is the exact moment that I had clarity for the first time in 2 months.

I was feeling numb, almost pleasantly numb, until those flowers were placed in my lap. At that exact instant when those soft waxy petals made contact with my hand, like a baby's skin being felt by her mom for the first time, I abruptly, instantaneously came out of my fog. I realized what I had just done. An overwhelming feeling of anguish and **death** and darkness crashed down on me with the force of an earthquake or an avalanche.

I knew that the intention of giving me flowers was to comfort me but it had the exact opposite effect. Never before had such a small act of kind-hearted intentions backfired so severely. It was in those seconds and then minutes that I knew I could never take back my awful and selfish mistake. What had I just done?

They say the only things that are guaranteed in life are death and taxes. I know with 1000% certainty that I will carry this burden, this heaviness and emptiness with me for my entire life. I know this feeling of loss and regret will never leave me. The misery, heartbreak, mourning, sadness, and guilt in my heart will never go away. I took away my child's chance to be born, to have a life, to live out their life. I'm the mother; I was supposed to protect my baby—that was my job as a mother.

As I was leaving the doctor's office 4 months ago after a prolonged and exceptionally painful migraine, no one thought to give me flowers on the way out the door. When I left the emergency room at St. Peter's Hospital last year after a car accident, not a single rose was offered to me. After I was "gifted" with that bouquet following my "procedure," it was as if everyone in that doctor's office was trying to convince me that my abortion was not such a bad thing, not the end of the world. It **was** the end of the world for my child. I know that doctors and nurses are trained to treat and diagnose without placing judgment, but I felt like that is exactly what they did with the flowers. The staff believes that abortions are ok (why else would they work there), but the flowers SCREAMED—it's not ok but we're trying to make you think it is. It's just how I felt at that moment and I still feel the same today.

I know in my gut that what I did was wrong. I am not writing to get anyone to agree or disagree with me. I'm simply telling my story. I believed in my mind, at that time, there was nothing wrong with having the "proce-dure." I didn't even have to try and convince myself it was an acceptable option. I didn't once try to justify my decision to abort my child. I had no problem with it until after it was over. I thought I could not face the realities of having a baby by myself. What I absolutely can't handle is the everlasting knowledge that I actually ended a life, a life that had started and had grown inside of me. You aren't handed flowers after a cavity, so why are they trying to console patients by making this gesture if it's not a nefarious act? The whole experience caused me to come to grips with the truth—I had just killed my baby. I took away something that belonged to my own child—their right to live, to exist.

The flowers were only part of the setting. Pleasant, soothing music was softly heard from every room, the walls were brightly colored, accents of floral wallpaper were everywhere, the aroma was vanilla, and the linens were warm and soft. Why shouldn't the clinic make their environment pleasant? There is absolutely nothing wrong with that. Problem is no amount of ambience can mask the reality of what just happened—the death of a life, my own baby's life.

I know many who read this might dismiss my story because they are staunchly pro-choice. I almost didn't agree to write down my story because of that fact. I'm certainly not here to engage in political debate. I never really had much of an opinion on the topic until I was faced with the decision. Yes, hard to believe but it's true. I honestly never thought I would be in a position where I had to make that decision. When I found out I was pregnant I was happy to have a legal and safe option so at that moment, yes, I was pro-choice. I did not know, nor could I have predicted, however, how I would feel in the aftermath. When those flowers were pressed into my hand, I had clarity for the first time in 51 days. Maybe I can blame fear, selfishness, or the hormones, or not being in a good relationship, for my decision, but it's crystal clear to me now. I did not expect to have so much guilt, sheer anguish, gloominess, and regret and it happened when they brought me flowers. I firmly believe, I know, that we really don't know how we will react or how we are going to feel until we are put in a specific situation. Would you run into a burning building to save someone? Most people wouldn't know the answer to that question unless they were put into that situation.

I didn't write my story to make a political point or to take a side in the abortion debate. I don't want people to think that I'm judging them or telling them what to do with their life. The whole purpose in sharing my story is to warn women that they **must** consider the possibility of living a **lifetime** with tremendous, overwhelming regret. I wish I had thought about how I would feel before I made the decision that I did. I made what I thought was a logical and informed decision, but I never took into account the emotional toll of what would transpire. I felt like I was literally in a dream state when I found out I was pregnant. It was kind of like being buzzed; I couldn't think straight. It seemed like such a quick and easy way to solve my "problem." Today I even get angry with myself for calling my unborn infant a "problem." Nothing is quick or easy about the decision I made. Of course there are women out there who have had abortions and did not feel at all like I did, women who have no regrets at all. I also know there are women out there like me who have aborted their babies and regretted it for the rest of their lives. Even Nicky Minaj, who is a pro-choice woman, has publicly stated that she regrets her abortion.

A few close friends have told me that I need therapy. I guess we could all benefit from some. I have insomnia. Some nights I lay awake thinking about all the reasons people give flowers: an anniversary, weddings, Valentine's Day, birthdays, actual birth days, and funeral too yes, but mostly flowers are given to celebrate a happy event and love. Why does the clinic give flowers to women who just aborted their babies? It's not a celebratory event.

These days still I love spring and summer. I dread the winter, particularly after Christmas when there are two more months of bitter cold weather and where so many days are gray and reminiscent of that day at the clinic. My mom would make sure to have forsythia bushes planted in the yard in all three houses we lived while growing up. They were always the first flowers to bloom in early spring, bright and sunshine yellow. When I was younger I remember seeing those yellow pedals emerge from the dark soil in my parent's backyard and thinking to myself that I've made it through another cold winter and the beautiful warm weather is coming. Decades have gone by and I still lose my breath every single year at the sight of those first yellow buds poking through in early spring. Those forsythia buds seem so vulnerable and fragile. One late cold snap and they won't survive.

I wonder what event or symbol would have woken me up somewhere down the road if that nurse hadn't handed me the flowers on the way out the door. I know that it would have been something else a week or a month later. Maybe seeing a baby play in the park or shopping for a friend's baby shower, or witnessing the birth of my niece. That was another very hard day for me. I never knew that day, nor could I have ever guessed, how I would feel when it was over. In my dreams I sit in my window seat, staring out and waiting for the forsythia bushes to bloom with my baby girl on my lap telling her grandma always planted them too. For some reason, I just know she was a girl. I dream that I'm back on that grim, sad day at the clinic where I decided to keep her instead of going through with the procedure. I leave the clinic with her in my belly instead of flowers.

Joe: Listen to Me!!!!!

There are not many places more uncomfortable for a man to be than a waiting room of an OB/GYN office. My eyes are darting around the room to the very young lady/girl across from me. I wonder if her parents know she is here. I see a half a dozen pregnant women like my wife, and wonder if they are married. My wife had to take off her wedding ring because her fingers are swollen so it's impossible to tell. Some of the faces look joyful while others make me wonder if they are expecting the worst. Are they about to get a disturbing diagnosis like I did last year?

I look to grab a magazine to distract myself but *Glamour* and *Good Housekeeping* aren't viable options for me to even pretend I am interested in. The useless 50-inch TV screen keeps replaying a looped message on good vs. bad cholesterol; at least I finally know the difference between HDL and LDL. I look past the young woman with tears in her eyes and spot a binder on the table labeled "I Wish I Knew." I am so eager for a distraction that I almost involuntarily reach for it. I panic, what if it is an instruction manual on giving birth?

I started to read the personal stories of my wife's doctor's patients. I read about Courtney and McKenzie and Rebecca. I picture their faces as I continue on. Do these stories match up to some of the women I've made awkward eye contact with in this very room?

After reading the journal, I felt as if a higher power had been speaking directly to me. I knew it was no coincidence that I was at the doctor's office with my wife that day, sitting directly in front of the coffee table with the patient journal in front of me. This doctor has two offices and typically pregnant women don't wait long, if at all, in the waiting room. I believe there is a reason that I picked up that journal. I have tried to make my wife's doctor appointments but because of work have been able to attend few. I felt an immediate sense of purpose, a mission if you may, to play my part in this aim to educate and prevent tragedy.

I made two promises, pledges really, to my children and to myself after reading Dr. Thompson's coffee table book. My first pledge is that my children will be educated on the topic of sex so that they don't have to learn these things the hard way, the way many of the women in this book had to. I promise to my son and to my daughter that I will be a source of information no matter how awkward or uncomfortable it makes me feel. I will provide the information that won't be taught in school, so that my children acquire all of the knowledge they need before they begin making decisions regarding their own sexuality. Feeling uncomfortable, uneasy or even downright embarrassed will not stop me from possibly saving their lives. I will do everything in my power to make sure my children will never write their own chapter in this book. I read the journal entries from Rebecca and Courtney and those passages really spoke to me. Parenting is hard, very hard. I don't judge other parents; we are all trying out best. I can promise that my kids will not look back at their parents, like McKenzie, and wonder why we never told them to wait and what's at stake if they don't. I can't fathom how Courtney's parents feel. I pray they don't batter themselves because they themselves didn't understand that their daughter could die from being uninformed and die from having sex. I will not fail to educate my kids on what may prove to be one of the most valuable things we can teach them, how to stay safe and alive. In the end, it's more important than their math and SAT scores and soccer skills. It MUST be discussed.

My next pledge—I decide to write my own personal account. As unfortunate as it might be, this ledger is more complete and informative than anything I have ever read. Our children must be made aware of the cold hard reality that many of these stories shed light on. But something is still missing—a male's perspective. That's why I've chosen to write my own story and send it to the doctor to be the first voice of the men.

Considering myself a masculine figure, I guess I have always shielded away from sharing the details of my private life. In this instance, revealing my story outweighs my nature to be private regarding such personal matters. I am the only child of a single mother. I never knew my father. Mom did **everything** for me and we were always very close. It was just the two of us for a very long time. Mom worked long hours to provide for us and she made sure I received a good education and that I valued the gift of higher education, faith in God, and family. I took my studies very seriously. I wasn't much of a partier in college; how could I slack off when my mother was working two jobs to make sure I got a chance to attend classes each semester. I wanted to make her proud and eventually be able to give back to her financially, since she had given me everything and sacrificed so much for me.

Because I was so dedicated to my academic career, I had little time for a social life or for girls. Well that, and I was also shy and slightly overweight, which made conversations with members of the opposite sex even more difficult. My mother always told me that one day a very smart and reputable woman would realize that I was a good, decent, kind, intelligent, hardworking man with an education and a good job, and that she would not let me get away. In the long run, as usual, Mom was right. In the short term, I slimmed down, graduated, matured, started making money, and women became attracted to me. It's not like I suddenly had dozens of girlfriends overnight, but I did meet and date a few women before I met my wonderful wife.

I was intelligent enough to know that no prophylactic is 100% effective. One of my fears, absolutely my biggest, was getting a woman pregnant before

I was married and ready to be a father. I was not going to bring a child into the world without an intact family—a mother and a father, married. I've experienced the pain of not having a father around; I never knew mine. I did not want to disappoint my mother either. I had a few women in my life as I mentioned before, and I was sexually active, but I often preferred oral sex to intercourse because I **thought** it was safer. There was no risk of an unplanned pregnancy with oral sex, which, I foolishly thought, solved all of my concerns and anxieties. Wow…this is hard to write down and share, but I'm going to do the best I can to contribute to Dr. Thompson's goal. As difficult as it is for me to open up about a very embarrassing subject, I'm writing this for my kids, my grandkids, and everyone who reads this and can learn from my mistake.

Jump forward 15 years later. I am happily married. My wonderful wife and I have a beautiful daughter and we are expecting another baby. I am literally living **The American Dream**, which is a very big deal for the son of a single mom and an immigrant from Ecuador. I have a good job, make enough money to live comfortably (few people can say that today), and even make enough money to put some in the bank. I love my job, own a house that truly feels like a home, and my wife and I are growing our family. My life seemed perfect until one day that little six-letter word crept into my world—CANCER.

So many people get cancer from bad habits like smoking or eating unhealthily. When I hear or read about the death of someone I consider young, I am often relieved when I find out they were doing something deleterious to their health like drinking and driving, being extremely over-weight, doing drugs, or smoking. But sometimes, people who get diagnosed with cancer or some other equally horrible disease are just plain unlucky. I was diagnosed with throat cancer but had never smoked a day in my life. I assumed I was just another unlucky casualty. I believed I had never done anything to expose myself to the risks of cancer. After all, I was way too intelligent and health conscious to smoke or chew tobacco; I never lived with or even dated a smoker. I was wrong. I did put myself at risk. I just didn't know it then.

My initial reaction was that of denial: perhaps my doctor had misdiagnosed me, perhaps the test was flawed, it simply cannot be true. "It's impossible," I kept telling my wife and myself. It took me about two days for my brain to process what I was told by my physician. I did expose myself to cancer. I did put myself at risk. I did jeopardize my life, my family, my future, and my children's future. I may leave them without a Dad. Although I did not **knowingly** expose myself, **that changes nothing**. Whether I knew what I was doing or not does not change my reality today. What you don't know can most definitely hurt you, even kill you.

If a drug addict injects himself with a used needle, he knows it's dangerous, but ultimately cannot stop himself because of his or her addiction. Still, in my mind, he knows the risks and has made a choice. I was informed, after my diagnosis, that throat cancer is not only caused by smoking, secondhand smoke, and chewing tobacco, but also by the Human Papilloma Virus or HPV. HPV is a sexually transmitted disease that can be transmitted genitally through intercourse and also through oral sex. HPV causes cervical cancer in women; I knew that. What I did not know was that it also can cause cancer in other areas including the vagina, vulva, penis, anus, tongue, and tonsils. It makes sense. I'd just never thought about it. HPV grows on epithelial cells which are found in the cervix, vagina, anus, penis, throat, and inside of the mouth. If it can grow in all of these places, of course it can cause cancer in all of these areas as well. Why can't the same virus, which is transmitted through skin-on-skin contact, be transmitted ways other than intercourse? It can.

My whole life I've believed in always doing the right thing. I believe in being honest, working hard, keeping the Sabbath day, living clean, and playing by the rules. I spent my youth avoiding cigarettes, drugs, drinking too much, and being with the wrong type of women. I avoided everything that I knew to be hazardous to my body and my mind. Now, at the age of 38, I find out that an insignificant relationship I had years ago with a woman who is now completely out of my life has the power to take away everything from me and my family—my life. Now this expired and uninspired relationship has the power to take a father away from his children, a husband away from his wife, a son away from his mother, the power to deliver a death sentence.

I am lucky, and grateful, and thankful to God because I am now in remission. I will always worry about the cancer coming back and what that will mean for my family. I have known people who have "beaten cancer" only to have it come back with a vengeance several years later. I cannot even increase my life insurance now to protect them further because of my diagnosis. I have to live the rest of my days like a criminal on the run, looking over my shoulder, always worrying when or if my past will come back to haunt me and my family. I worry every day that it will come back even though today I am cancer-free. It's like walking through life with a black cloud over your head. Is it going to rain down on me tomorrow, next month, in three years?

I regret being with other women before my wife. It absolutely, unequivocally was not worth the pain, worry, and stress it caused my family and me. There is a reason God's way is to wait for marriage. Cancer has caused physical pain and emotional pain to me and everyone around me. I deeply resent the fact that I was not educated on the risks I was taking. I wish I had educated myself more effectively; I wish had come across something like this journal 15 years ago.

I am an educated, well-read, informed, and intelligent man. I have a bachelor's and a master's degree, but they don't teach you everything you need to know in school. I never heard anywhere in school, in the news, in books, etc. that I could get cancer from oral sex. I just wasn't reading the right books. No one ever told me that one unimportant fling (I don't even define it as a relationship now) could come back over a decade later and **steal my life from me**. If you too do not know this, I am glad you are reading my very painful story. Please share my story with your friends. My children will know the risks and the facts before they ever decide to have oral sex. Tell your friends, your kids, your family members. Tell everyone you know that oral sex is not safe.

It is not an easy subject to discuss and it can be very nerve-racking and anxiety-provoking, but leaving your children in the dark is a much more difficult reality to face than an uncomfortable conversation. When my children have reached the right age, I plan to inform them of the dangers of drugs, alcohol, smoking, drinking and driving, unprotected sex, and oral sex. Parents, add another topic to that list—talk to them about the dangers of oral sex. Make sure they know that one moment in their lives, one encounter, one relationship (or night) that you believe will last but often doesn't, can change their lives. We need to put oral sex on the list of things we educate our kids about. Thank you for reading my story.

Lissa: Mended

I'm not a writer. Dr. Thompson told me not to worry about that. The story is what matters. She is my OB/GYN but she did not diagnose me. My dentist did. I had a small lump below my jaw. My dentist found it during a routine teeth cleaning. I had oral cancer. I went through chemo and radiation and had surgery. It was hellish—the nausea, sores in my mouth, extreme fatigue, dozens of doctor visits, and hair loss.

My case is unusual because men are more likely to get oral cancer than women by 4 to 1. Men are less likely to clear the HPV infection on their own. I get a Pap smear annually but there is no such preventative measure for oral cancer. The HPV vaccine would have helped but I was too old to get it when it came out.

As painful as the chemo treatments were, losing my hair was absolutely horrible. I felt ugly and unattractive. I didn't want to leave my house, so I rarely did. I didn't like the attention I would get even with a hat or scarf on. I'm not a girl that spends a lot of time on hair and makeup, but I was typically satisfied with my appearance after a quick ten-minute routine of foundation and mascara. Having no hair changes your appearance and self-esteem. Then, after suffering all of that, I was told I had to have surgery on my jaw, my face.

The cancer spread pretty fast so part of my jaw had to be removed. My face is now asymmetrical and there is a 3-inch scar that you can't miss. I can try to have a plastic surgeon correct it but it will never be the same. I will never look like I did before the surgery. I have to look at my face every day and it's a constant source of sadness, even disgust, and sometimes, often truthfully, tears. Right now I don't have the money for plastic surgery.

Oral cancer from HPV is harder to find than oral cancer from tobacco use because the HPV-caused cancer has fewer symptoms. Twenty-six million Americans have an oral HPV infection. People have HPV for years, even decades before it is found. HPV, not tobacco use, is the number one reason for cancer of the tonsils and tongue. Even though more men get oral cancer from HPV, women are more likely to get HPV from a fewer number of partners. Oral cancer is growing fastest in healthy non-smoking 35–55-year-olds (who probably contracted it at a much younger age). There are almost 200 strains of HPV—nine cause cancer and six more are suspected to cause cancer.

I don't know what else to say. All this information is available online. I never thought I would or could get oral cancer from sex that I probably had years and years ago. Chemotherapy is the most miserable thing I could imagine at the time. It is really, really awful how sick it makes you feel. Looking at my face is worse. I don't let people take pictures of me and would have thrown away every mirror in my house if I could pluck my eyebrows without one. Maybe I should start getting someone to do the threading on me.

What happened to me is sort of rare but it happened. Kind of like hitting the lottery—it's rare but it happens to people. When I was in school I remember reading a short story "The Lottery." Someone was randomly picked every year to be stoned to death by the rest of the town. I feel like somehow I got picked at random. Why? Unlike the fictional story I had to read in school, I could have prevented it but I didn't know.

I did have several sexual partners in my life. I was molested as a kid, which messed me up for a while. I thought it was ok to have sex with anyone I found attractive because it was no longer something special between two people in love. I feel differently now, but I didn't get through that period of my life unscathed. I'm not sure where this story is going. I'm just writing. I guess I want to tell other girls that if you were abused or raped, don't let that change your behavior. An experience like that definitely changes your thinking but it should never change your behavior like it did mine. I believed that sex was no big deal after my abuse. I regret the way I thought about what happened to me at that time, but I didn't tell anyone so I just had myself to listen to. I regret thinking that I possible encouraged this awful incident to happen to me as a 12-year-old, and I regret my actions afterward and not just because I got cancer. Unfortunately, it's a pretty common way of thinking particularly at a very young age—somehow it's our fault.

One of my friends who had a similar experience to mine sometimes describes herself as "damaged." This makes me so sad; actually it makes me angry at times. It really BOTHERS me. No one gets through this life unscathed. **I'm not damaged**. I'm just a person who went through a bad experience like millions of others walking this earth. I also don't describe myself as a survivor. Most will disagree with me but it was never life or death to me, just a very bad thing to happen. Surviving to me conjures up people literally surviving a life or death situation like the Holocaust. I look at the positive—I'm alive, now healthy, and everything else in my life is good.

My advice—just please think before you do anything, particularly involving having any type of sex. People do get over sex abuse. I was able to put it behind me. Make sure you are not having sex for the wrong reasons. There are plenty of wrong reasons and only a few right reasons.

Tori: Why Not Me?

They say, "The pen is mightier than the sword." That is the purpose behind Dr. Thompson's coffee table book. I hope there is a copy of this book on every coffee table in America. The reason I agreed to share my story, my experience is because I do believe that knowledge and information, and more specifically, interpreting and utilizing that information is indeed a powerful tool we should pass along. I've read the tragic stories of the other women in this book, and I'm ready to share my own experience. I am 32 years old, and I am a registered nurse. I was not a teenager when I got an STD like many of the other patients in this journal. I was well into adulthood, and a healthcare professional. I should have known better. As a nurse, I see firsthand the need and the benefits of medications and vaccinations. But I also see an even greater need for information to prevent disease and unplanned pregnancy.

I have treated patients with STDs. Actually today the politically correct term is STIs—sexually transmitted infections. The play on words is not lost on me. "Infections" has a gentler ring than "disease," but that doesn't diminish the term's meaning. I guess it's not supposed to sound so bad. "It's just an infection." Medications are given to cure the disease, lessen the symptoms, or even decrease the risk of spreading the disease to your partner. Today we even have vaccines to prevent getting some of the diseases. We have access to drugs and vaccines that were not available a generation or so ago, when STIs were thought to be running rampant. Guess what? The number of STIs has actually **increased** rapidly in the last several years. The reason?

Maybe we think that because of these new advances we are safer than ever. I really don't know the answer. I do know however that none of these new discoveries in medicine can compare in effectiveness to knowledge when it comes to preventing the complications and side effects of having sex.

I am a realist. I do not believe that you can stop people from having sex with multiple partners, stop casual sex, or stop teens and others from having unprotected sex. (**Unprotected sex seems to indicate that there is such a thing as protected sex, which is not really true. Protected sex really means safer sex but not entirely safe.**) If you look at trends and statistics, you will notice that fewer and fewer people get married today and there is a high rate of divorce. We get married at an older age, and there is a tremendous increase in people having kids outside of marriage compared to earlier generations. We are not all going to wait until we are married to have sex, and not all of us will get married. Again, I am a realist and I believe that we can, through discussion and attention to the subject, educate teens, single people, divorced people going back into the dating scene, and anyone and everyone else that the consequences of sex can be severe and devastating. These consequences can include things much worse than pregnancy, crabs, or genital lesions that go away. Some STIs have much, much graver outcomes.

I understand that people still drink and drive knowing what can happen. They still smoke fully aware of the risk of cancer and lung disease. They do drugs after being taught time and time again the risk of sickness, addiction, and even death. Fewer people smoke cigarettes today vs. several years back because we all know the risks. My 10-year-old nephew can list not only some of the 200 poisons in cigarettes (including rat poison which I did not know) but also the side effects: yellow teeth and fingers, heart disease, wrinkles, bad breath, dizziness, COPD, throat cancer, lung cancer, shortness of breath, etc. Imagine teens being able to spout out the long list of STIs, their prevalence, and their consequences such as infertility, cancer, genital ulcers, miscarriages, and death. Imagine a decrease in STIs instead of an increase year after year because more and more of us are educated on the risks, the facts. Would kids reduce the number of partners they had in a lifetime if they knew how dangerous sex can be? We should treat these activities with the same caution and attention that they deserve like we do with drug addiction and driving under the influence of alcohol.

If you drive by the back entrance of the hospital I work at, you will see a group of 4–5 nurses at any given time smoking. I know why they smoke even though they know how deadly smoking can be. Nurses work long 10–12-hour shifts and don't get regularly scheduled lunches or breaks. Smoking controls your appetite and it's also a stress reliever. I guess I know why my coworkers smoke but I really don't understand it—we know better or we should. I never saw my sex life as particularly self-destructive, but it was and I should have known better. It's not like I'm recalling the statistics on new cases of gonorrhea in the U.S. when I'm working a shift at my hospital.

I need to make a quick point about who else, besides teens, needs to be clear on the unforeseen dangers of sex. This book is really directed at teens; however, it is also essential reading for adults, and in particular, divorced women for two basic reasons. The first reason is because many adults will have their own babies who will one day grow into teens that need to be educated by their parents, because unfortunately they likely won't be told this information in their schools. The second reason is the chance of divorce. With a 50% divorce rate often quoted in the U.S., many married folks end up divorced and eventually single again and jumping back into the dating pool. When you are a 30-something, 40-something, or 50-something and single, there are few, if any, peers in your dating pool that do not have an ex, and therefore a sexual history to share, literally, with you.

I have a 37-year-old divorced friend who at 22 years old married her high school sweetheart. Long story short, they divorced, and after 3 years of grieving and adjusting to being on her own, Linda is looking to date again. I fully support her, but there is only one problem; this woman knows nothing on the subject of men, sex, dating today, and how they fit together. She has lived in a bubble for too long and has not been properly informed about what is out there lurking as far as diseases transmitted through all types of sexual contact. I had to set her straight, and I am glad I did. She never had to worry about sexually transmitted diseases before so she didn't know what she didn't know. You should have seen her face when I told her some of the real-life stories from Dr. Thompson's book. She is dating a great guy now, but I guarantee you she took it slow. A divorced mom needs this book as much as her teenage daughter does, so if you are a teenage girl reading this and your mom is single, get a copy of this journal to her!

So as promised, this is my story. This is not something I witnessed as a nurse. This is me. I am a single 32-year-old woman who works crazy hours and long shifts. I've had a few serious relationships but have not come close to finding a man I would consider marrying. I live alone and date. I do not "sleep around" or "hook up." I've only had one one-night stand in my life. I never thought my behavior was putting me on a pathway to getting an STI but if I gave the subject of my risk factors five minutes of serious thought, then maybe I could have predicted my future. Even those of us who know the risks don't really like to think about them. I've heard it said to me hundreds of times in the emergency room, "I didn't think this would ever happen to me." Then I caught myself saying those same words when I got diagnosed. I REALLY didn't think it would happen to me. It did. I should not have been surprised.

I think condom manufacturers should put STI facts on the wrapper, kind of like Snapple Facts. You open the box and the label reads, "3 out of 5 Americans have herpes." We all, collectively, regardless of age or circumstance I guess, need to be reminded over and over again—it can happen to you. Maybe the condoms should have a message like a fortune cookie.

I just got a fortune cookie that said, "Avoid taking unnecessary gambles." It's true!!!

My story does not by any means compare to many of the others stories you have read, but it is just as real and horrible to me. I have PID or Pelvic Inflammatory Disease. It took several months to get diagnosed, which is common for what I have. In fact 70% to 80% of people with PID have no symptoms for months, sometimes even years. It's called the "silent epidemic." The first sign that something was wrong was the fact that I had to urinate constantly. This became a big problem because of my profession. Sometimes you just can't leave a patient and my coworkers—the nurses, nurses' aides, and the doctors at my hospital—were getting annoyed with me because of my frequent breaks. At first, my doctor thought it was possibly stress-related. Nursing is very stressful, particularly at a large hospital with a high volume of patients. Next, I developed frequent stomachaches and cramps. After weeks of those symptoms and an increasing intensity in my pain, I began to worry. Then I started bleeding. I knew something was wrong.

I was finally diagnosed with chlamydia. When chlamydia or gonorrhea go undiagnosed for a period of time and are untreated, the person can develop PID. I had suffered months of pain, anxiety, problems with job performance, which affected my patients, a negative performance review at work, stress, not to mention no sex. I was fearful that I might lose my job because the symptoms persisted for so long. I could not focus on my work because of my pain and stress. I felt like I was letting my patients down because I could not focus on them the way I used to, the way I should.

I ended up having to be admitted to my hospital and was given IV antibiotics when the pain was so severe I could no longer stand. I would have gone to another hospital if I did not get sick at work. Now some of my coworkers were aware that I had chlamydia, so my pain was compounded by embarrassment.

After the first minute of shock and denial that I had PID due to untreated chlamydia, I said to myself, "Why not me?" instead of the usual "Why is this happening to me?" I've been working in a hospital in a major city for over 7 years and have seen quite a bit of trauma, disease, and death. No one deserves to be paralyzed from a car accident, or to be bedbound at the age of 40 wearing a diaper because of MS, or to lose both your legs due to diabetes. I haven't seen it all, but I've seen enough to be thankful that I can get out of bed every day and walk across the floor. I am thankful every day that I know and recognize my family members and am not devastated by a traumatic brain injury or Alzheimer's disease. I try to remember to be grateful every day because I can feed myself, bathe myself; I can see, hear, speak, and earn a living. I see people every day who have lost their independence due to disease. Nursing teaches you to count the blessings of health every day.

It could be worse for me, much, much worse. My patients remind me of that every day. My own personal tale is the least devastating of all the stories I have read in this book. I am thankful because my disease was a wakeup call for me to be more careful, to protect my health, to value my body, and to be much more discerning about who I sleep with. It was just not worth the pain, or the embarrassment, to be so careless. People never think it can happen to them. I hear this over and over again. Don't say to yourself, "It won't happen to me." Bad things happen to good people every second of every day. Yesterday I walked through the oncology floor where dozens of people of all ages come and go every day for IV chemotherapy. Instead, ask yourself, "Why not me?" and be safe. Protect your body. The fortune cookie was right; it's not worth the unnecessary gamble and trust me it's often a gamble.

Veronica: Boxer Shorts Condoms?

This shouldn't be happening to me. It just can't be real. I'm in honors classes. I'm smart. I've only been with one guy, and he has been my boyfriend for almost three years. How the hell did I get genital warts? We were so careful. We used a condom every single time. I'm not an idiot like those two girls walking around my high school trying to hide their bumps. It's not working, Dana and Morgan; **everyone knows you're pregnant**!! I'd see them walking through the halls and used to think to myself, "How can they be so dumb—to get pregnant in high school? Hello, use some protection!!!" Now I think, "OMG! That could have easily been me." I contracted genital warts. But how? I used protection, and I still got an STD.

Brad and I have never even had a close call like a condom falling off or breaking or anything like that. When I started to itch down there, I thought I had a urinary tract infection, because some of my friends have had that. I told Brad and asked him if he had any problems or symptoms or diseases he failed to tell me about and he said no, nothing.

I was so rude to Dr. Thompson when I came to see her. I even yelled at her and demanded she re-test me because she just made a big mistake. I was only with Brad. There is no one else. We used a condom every single time. She was very patient and very kind when she told me it is no mistake—I had genital warts. There was nothing physically there though, just itching and burning. She said they are not always visible. They may not have been visible on my boyfriend either. Brad probably didn't even know he had them. I just kept telling myself over and over again it's not possible. **This has to be a mistake.**

I went through all five stages of grieving in about 30 minutes. First, I was in denial. This is not happening to me. It is not possible that I have ruined my body with an STD. Dr. T must've made a huge mistake. I've only been with one guy!!! Next came the anger. My doctor is an idiot; how can she be so incompetent! That was followed by anger at Brad—how could he do this to me? Did he cheat on me? I am going to kill him. I absolutely tried to bargain with God. "Please God, let this be a mistake, please!!!!!!! I'll do anything. Things like this aren't supposed to happen to girls like me." I am not at all promiscuous, and I'm certainly not stupid. Then the sadness hit me. I wouldn't say I was depressed but I was really, really down. I'm diseased and I feel dirty and damaged; nothing can change that. I'm also upset because of the risk of cervical cancer. I read online that different HPV strains can cause either genital warts or cervical cancer. Now I have that to worry about, that too on top of everything else. Finally, I had no choice but to accept it. I'm not a virgin. I had sex with my boyfriend and that is how people get pregnant and get STDs. I was stupid to believe that I was any better than Dana or Morgan. Turns out I'm no better, no smarter. I just thought I was. I really did.

I asked Dr. Thompson, "How did this happen?" Yes, I did realize how silly that sounded immediately after the words left my lips **but we ALWAYS used a condom**!!!! Plus, my mother made me get vaccinated when I was 14. The vaccine is supposed to prevent HPV, cancer, and genital warts. Dr. T explained that HPV, like HSV (herpes simplex virus), is spread by skin-on-skin contact. So, if Brad had HPV (which he did) and the infected skin was not on his penis but somewhere in his "genital area," I was not protected. The infected skin was not under the condom, leaving me at risk. Condoms are actually more effective for diseases that are spread by fluids (semen) like HIV. Great. No one really worries about getting HIV.

I can't believe it—**Why didn't anyone tell us that**? She said that many people are infected but have no symptoms or "subclinical symptoms" like burning or itching but no lesions. Gross, I can't even believe I'm using these words. Brad has undetected HPV somewhere in his "genital region," which was not physically or literally under the condom, so it spread to me. He could have been contagious on his testicles or even his upper thigh or lower abdomen (yes, I know this is disgusting but there is no other way to tell this story, sorry). My doctor told me that he would need to wear a condom **in the shape of boxer shorts** to protect me from STDs transmitted through skin-on-skin contact. What? Boxer shorts–shaped condoms! News flash—they don't exist. Have you ever heard of that before? No, you most likely haven't, which is why I agreed to write this story in her book of love gone wrong, ok really sex gone wrong. Now you know. Don't be naïve like I was and don't be so trusting of boys. Oh, and by the way, I wasn't Brad's first like he'd told me on many occasions, so please make sure you trust, I mean really trust, your partner before getting into bed with him. And even then, make him get tested! And then ask to see the test results!!

Now I'm back to Stage II of my grieving process: anger. I am really, really pissed off. Why did I learn all of this information **after it was too late**? I sat in health class all year long and no one ever told us any of this. Specifically when I say "this," I mean about the genital area being contagious, condoms being less effective in stopping the spread of skin-to-skin diseases vs. diseases transmitted through fluids, and the whole boxer shorts condom concept and that the vaccine is not 100% effective. We got the usual talk on drugs, vaping, pregnancy, and even sunbathing, but no one ever told me or my other 380 classmates that we could get an STD even when using protection. Why not?? When we were putting condoms on bananas no one said, "By the way it's only going to prevent diseases that are on the banana, nowhere else." I still don't know why the powers-that-be decided not to tell us EVERYTHING we need to know. I already know that smoking is dangerous—**how about teaching us something we don't already know for a change**? Why are they still teaching us about this stuff in high school? We all went through DARE in the fifth grade. We really needed to know this **other** stuff. **I really needed to know**. I listened. I didn't smoke or do drugs. If someone would've told me about HPV and that I can easily get it even with a condom, I would have listened as well. Some of us teens do listen, you know!

I read online that 80% of women will get HPV in their lifetime, yet no one, not the Board of Education, not the people who set the curriculum, not the federal government who puts out public service announcements think that teens need to know that you can get the most common STD (the one that can cause cancer too; I read about Rebecca) even with a condom. What the hell is going on? This needs to be addressed and corrected.

To this day, I'm still overwhelmed with rage when I think about it. I mean, how many of my classmates got HPV too and then got cancer? We should be outraged. Why are the adults in charge telling us to practice safe sex when safe sex can still get us sick, really sick? Do they think we are so dumb that we just won't listen, that we can't understand the facts? Do they even know the facts? Some politicians want to allow 16-year-olds to vote now. Well, if you are going to expect us to know enough to vote, then you better not sugarcoat the truth from us. It's bad enough to not teach us what we need to know, but to actually teach us that condoms are the answer is so irresponsible. Maybe I should sue somebody.

I thought I was Brad's first. I was wrong. He lied. He was my first. He eventually told me that he had sex with one other girl before me but he didn't want me to get mad. He said it was only one time and he didn't love her. If that's true, then he was definitely not her first. This disease had to come from somewhere. That means that I am exposed to the sexual history, including the diseases, of Brad, his ex, and her exes (unknown number) at a minimum. Who knows at this point who is telling the truth? Maybe his ex-girlfriend had a partner or two or more before meeting Brad. The bottom line is I've been exposed to the diseases of an **unknown** amount of people. I swear I start to itch when I just think about that.

I had a dream that I marched down to the next Board of Education meeting and demanded that Dr. Thompson teach sex education from now on. Of course, I'm not going to do that because that would expose me. Maybe that's why no one talks to teens about the truth, because they've all found out the hard way too. Dr. Thompson seems as frustrated as I am because so many of her patients are **just like me**. The least I can do is write my chapter along with all the others in her waiting room book. I hope you learn from the mistakes of others.

I know Dr. T is a very busy doctor and had a waiting room full of other patients to see but she took the time and asked me a question. I told her my biggest concern, before the STD, was getting pregnant. She asked me how effective I thought condoms were for preventing pregnancy. I told her I read the box (I told you I'm no dummy); it said 98% to 99%. I did my research. She asked me what that means. I was really confused by this. She said, "Veronica, think, really think about my question—you are a smart girl." I started to think very hard but I still came up with nothing. Then she gave me a clue. She said,

% = 100

Immediately the light bulb went off above my head. It really did, just like that. I knew where she was going. Do you get it? Ok, if you don't, I'll explain.

Ninety-nine percent sounds really good to me, like one in a million or at least like one in 100,000 times condoms are used they fail. But % means 100 so once or twice in 100 uses, condoms will not prevent pregnancy. It doesn't sound so good now, not so effective, not at all foolproof like I assumed, **like I was counting on**. One or two times in 100, condoms are not getting the job done. That is so scary to me. It should be to you too.

There are approximately 1600 students in my high school. Let's assume that half are female, and that of those 800, another half will have sex before they graduate. If all or most of us are using condoms or birth control pills, which also claim to be 99% effective, then about 4 of these girls will get pregnant. I was not as safe as I thought I was. Maybe Dana and Morgan thought they were being safe too. If the lunch lady in our cafeteria told us that 4 of the 500 lunches being served today were going to cause food poisoning, I would pass on lunch that day. I never really thought that deeply about what the statistics really meant, about what I didn't know. It's no surprise that two of my classmates are expecting babies in the next few months.

Brad and I broke up. For some crazy reason, I believed that he did not know he had HPV. Maybe he lied, maybe he told the truth. He lied to me about his ex, so I can never fully trust him. I spent my freshman year of college going back and forth to the doctor to get tested and treated for months. I am one of the lucky ones. I read about the girl in this book that did get cancer from HPV. That could've been me. I only had three outbreaks, which sucks, but again it could have been a lot worse.

Life goes on. We live and we learn. I at least have the courage to tell my new college friends and roommates about how dangerous sex can be. I don't want to be the mother hen in the group but they are having a lot of sex. No one told me, but I'm definitely going to tell them. They might thank me one day. I am not swearing off sex during my college years but I'm not hooking up with random guys either. I am only going to be with guys I'm in a relationship with. It's too risky to have multiple partners, one-night stands, or sex with anyone you don't really know well.

Pause

Think
(Long-term)

Decide
(With all the information you now have)

Is this really worth possible_____?
(Fill in the blank)

Pregnancy, infertility, genital disease, physical pain, lifelong disease, abortion, cancer, giving up your baby, genital sores and ulcers, future miscarriages, emotional pain, death?

Ryan: My Turn

I have two sisters and a girlfriend (**had** a girlfriend), so I know that girls have a type of female doctor they go to when they need birth control pills or when they have to have some female thing checked out. Some of the girls in high school go to a clinic downtown. I learned in health class that girls are statistically more at risk than guys for getting some STDs partly because more of their body surface area is exposed during sex, and partly because they are exposed to more fluids than a guy. But guys have a big disadvantage as well. We don't have a doctor we can visit before we have sex; we simply go to the nearest pharmacy and buy condoms. Well, at least some of us do.

If I had a doctor or clinic to go to, maybe I would have asked some questions, picked up a brochure in the waiting room, and found out some more information. Maybe I would have known what I didn't know, what I should have known, what I wish I had known. When I started high school I got psoriasis, which is a rash. It was on my legs and chest. My mom took me to the doctor. I never had it before. The doctor said that it was no big deal and gave me some cream to put on it. He told me it could have been from the stress of a new school, harder classes, etc.

When I was a junior I had another rash; this time on my upper thighs. I figured it was the same thing so I wasn't worried about it. I put the cream on it again and it went away. I guess it did look a little different but what do I know? I'm a guy. I don't pay close attention to these things. It never really crossed my mind that I should go to a doctor and have it checked out. I never thought in a million years that I had an STD. I have only been with a few girls, three if you need to know, and I always used condoms. The girls insisted on it. My girlfriend (ex-girlfriend now) Cassie got a rash too and she went to the gynecologist. She told me she had herpes and then she broke up with me.

It was definitely over. She wouldn't talk to me in school or anywhere else. We finally talked a few months later. She was still really pissed off. I was her first and only partner, so she knew it had to have been me who gave her herpes. I felt horrible about it, I still do, but I really, really didn't know I had it. Even her doctor told her that it was very possible that I had mild symptoms or perhaps no visible symptoms and I may not have known what I had. There was definitely no rash on me when we had sex. She said she didn't know what to believe and was so angry and sad and embarrassed about having an STD that she was not interested in being in any relationship right now. She said she could never really trust me again and I get it. She has a right to be mad but I just hope that she realizes one day that I didn't do it on purpose. I did not deceive her intentionally. I wouldn't do that to her or anyone else. I really never knew I had herpes. I really did, still do, love her; I would not have hid the STD from her if I knew I had it, NEVER.

I'm upset and pissed off too. My rash was not my psoriasis coming back. I have herpes, and I'll have this disease for the rest of my life. I will have to tell all future partners I have it (that isn't going to make me popular with girls), and I probably lost the love of my life because of herpes. We would still be together today if this didn't happen, but it wasn't entirely my fault.

Knowing that I'll have this disease forever really sucks too. I mean it won't be there every day; the rash comes and goes, but still, it's a shitty thing to deal with. I can't believe either Katie or Emily gave it to me. Who the hell have they been with? Could Cassie have given it to me? Did she lie about me being her first? I assumed that I was Katie's first and Emily's first but that obviously can't be true. This is such BS.

It's too late to go back and do things differently. I probably still would have had sex with the girls even if I knew; it's hard to say no when they are willing. I would have gone to a doctor if there was a doctor that guys went to. Are there doctors for guys? I still don't know. I wasn't going to risk going to our family doctor. I'm pretty sure they can't tell my parents but I'm not risking that and our family doctor has known me since I was about 8; it's just too weird. I guess the condoms don't work as well as we all think they do because we are all still passing around diseases to each other.

My friend Cody has a problem too and looked up his symptoms online. He said that there is a doctor for guys, a "urologist." Who knew? Oh hell, it's too late now. As my mom likes to say, "You can't put the toothpaste back in the tube." Man, is that ever true for me! I think it's pretty one-sided though. It seems to me that there are more doctors for girls to go to than there are for guys. If we had somewhere to go, maybe we would know more, get more information and treatment, and be less likely to pass STDs on to the girls. I don't think any teenage guys know to go to a urologist. Maybe my buddy Jim would finally go to the doctor and realize that his "zipper cut" is an STD too. If he really just had an unfortunate zipper accident, wouldn't it have healed 4 months after the incident? I'm just saying, what about the guys, where do we go? Who can treat us, diagnose us, help us, and educate us? We just slap on a condom and believe we're good to go. That's just not working for me now.

Jordan: Playing with Fire

Let me start by telling you that my story cannot be described as tragic or life-threatening. It is not nearly as sad or painful as the other girls' stories. Dr. T never even asked me to write a chapter in her book. My story was probably not dismal enough for her to consider it. It is, however, awful and life-altering to me. I asked Dr. T if I could contribute my own story to the book because I too have something to say.

I first visited Dr. Thompson when I was 15 years old. I was a freshman in high school and was missing school frequently because of extremely painful cramps whenever I got my period. I was always doubled over in pain and could not even go to school some days. She put me on birth control pills, which helped. I was an A student and want to be a pediatrician one day; missing school was not an option because I didn't want to fall behind. I didn't even have a boyfriend at the time; I was simply on the pill to alleviate the pain of my cramps.

I met my boyfriend, T.J., when we were both juniors. I sat behind him in chemistry class. I hadn't encountered him around our school before that class. I didn't know anything about him but he was really cute. He was tall, a good dresser, and had great hair. A lot of the boys in my school dressed really sloppy or just plain; they settled on jeans and an old, faded t-shirt every day. T.J. really stood out. He always looked like he could be in a magazine. My best friend, Emma, told me she could literally "feel sparks" between us when we were together. We definitely had chemistry, which is funny because we met in chemistry class.

T.J. and I were together for about 8 months when we had sex. This is where things started to get complicated. You see, we never planned on having sex that day or any other day, not at that time. I know 8 months is a long time by some kids' standards, but we were different. Some kids get a hotel room or plan some elaborate evening for their first time if their parents are out of town. It was not at all like that for us. T.J. and I were kind of similar I guess. A lot of my friends had sex with their boyfriends because the guys kind of pressured them. I don't at all mean they were forced; I just mean that they'd ask and ask and kind of wear down the girls. To be honest, many of my friends have sex with their boyfriends because they are afraid the guys will break up with them eventually if they don't do it. I feel bad for them; T.J. is not like that.

T.J. and I did have this crazy physical attraction between us but we both knew that there was always a chance of pregnancy even with protection, so we just decided not to go all the way. We thought there was no reason to; T.J. and I got **creative**. I mean there are lots of things you can do as a couple without having sex or even oral sex (that causes diseases too). We did just about everything but have intercourse or oral sex. Also, I read *Forever Is a Really Long Time* while waiting in my doctor's office. That is some scary shit. It was really the best of both worlds; we could fool around but not worry about diseases or me getting pregnant. T.J. said he was a virgin but I was super paranoid. I believed him, but how could I ever really know? Guys tend to lie. Again, I read the book and read about Veronica and Brad. We fooled around all the time at his parents' house after school. His parents never got home before 6 PM. It was perfect. There was no chance of pregnancy, disease, or getting caught by our parents.

T.J. and I were at his parents' house one night. They went out for "back to school" night for his little brother. The last few times we fooled around we decided to get completely naked, and then it just happened instinctually. Nothing was discussed or decided. No one ever said, "Let's have sex tonight."

We both just went too far that time. It was literally just one moment where we couldn't control our emotions and urges, and it happened. One moment, mere seconds, changed things forever. We had sex. We thought we were being so smart, so careful up to this point, but we were playing with fire.

After it was over, I felt really weird. I mean it felt great in that moment (really great) and all, but I was no longer a virgin. It was just a very strange feeling; I guess because it wasn't planned. I never thought about how I would feel afterward. I don't know, maybe all girls feel different after their first time. I felt strange and weird and a little overwhelmed, to be honest.

You know, I hear all the time from adults that they think most teenagers are all having oral sex at 14 years old and most teens are doing it. It's just not true, at least not in my circle of friends. I never thought I would be the first one in my group to have sex. My friends are still virgins. I didn't think I would be the first one to do it. I really wasn't ready. All of a sudden, I could not get these scary thoughts out of my head. I imagined that I became pregnant even though I was on the pill. I knew it could still happen. I was overwhelmed with **what ifs** and overwhelming, sometimes even panic-inducing, anxiety.

I went home that night and prayed my parents wouldn't be able to look at me and somehow just know. I felt like they could look at my face and know something was different, as if losing your virginity changed your entire complexion. Looking back on it, I was being a little paranoid. What can I say; it's just how I felt. I went to school the next day, but I couldn't concentrate. I was freaking out inside. I wanted a **do over** like when we were kids playing on the playground at school yelling "do over" if we missed the ball. I didn't mean to do it. I could have changed my life in that moment. I read the book. I know what can happen. I definitely failed my chemistry test in period 3. I was in a full state of panic by the fourth period and decided I had to go back to see Dr. Thompson and have her test me. I could've bought a pregnancy test at the pharmacy but that is so embarrassing and I probably wouldn't trust it. I also wanted to get tested for STDs. I couldn't stop thinking about all those girls in Dr. T's book. Was I going to be one of them? I was losing my mind. It wasn't logical but I couldn't rest until I got checked out. There was no way to drive out the paranoia until I saw the MD.

Dr. Thompson checked me out and I was so relieved when she told me I was fine, not pregnant. She tested me for STDs too. I had to wait for the results, which seemed like a very long time, but eventually I got the all clear, no diseases. It felt like a ton of bricks was lifted off my body. I know it may have made no sense to be so nervous, but I really couldn't think straight after we did it that one time. Thank you, God! I felt like I dodged a bullet. It only takes one time for something bad to happen. The whole experience was very stressful and as much as I did actually enjoy the sex, it just caused me way too much anxiety in the aftermath.

I was blowing off T.J. for the next several days after we had sex. I really didn't know what to say to him. I knew he wanted to do it again. I mean, what the heck; we were no longer virgins now. How could we go back to normal? I just knew myself, and I knew that I was too irrational and nervous but that's just me. That's who I am, and I realized I just wasn't emotionally ready for all the stuff that came with having sex. Perhaps my body was ready but not my mind. I didn't know what to say to him. I mean, who does it one time and never again!

I was trying to figure out what to tell him and trying not to let all this drama distract me from school and homework but the worst was yet to come. I though the storm had passed. I was wrong. I came home from school a few weeks later and my dad was home. He never gets home early but he had a meeting that day and got home at 4 PM. He decided to open the mail. I don't think I've ever seen my dad open the mail before. He was sitting at the kitchen table with a pile of papers and ripped envelopes in front of him. He looked different, sadder than usual. I could tell something was wrong. Did he know from looking at my face? What the hell came in the mail? I think he knows. He looked heartbroken.

Do you know what an EOB is? It's an Explanation of Benefits. Every time you go to the doctor, your insurance company sends you a statement that includes dates of service, how much your co-pay is, how much the insurance company pays, and what was done in the office. It includes an ICD 10 Code and a CPT code. These are standard codes for billing. They can be looked up online and will tell you the diagnosis, for example, the flu, and the codes can tell what was done in the office, for example, STD screening or getting stitches. I really wish I knew this before. I was so stupid. I thought that if I paid the $30.00 co-pay in cash, my parents would never find out I went to see Dr. Thompson on my own. There it was in black and white for my poor dad to read. His daughter was tested for STDs and had a pregnancy test. I wanted to die. It was so embarrassing and shameful. No, I didn't have a horrible disease and I wasn't pregnant, but my dad finding out that I'd been sleeping with my boyfriend was pretty devastating to me. I then recognized what that look on his face was—absolute disappointment. I wanted to tell him it was a mistake and that we never did it again. I knew he'd never believe that even though it was the truth.

My mom and I were like oil and water for the next couple of months. She drove me crazy almost every day keeping track of my daily movements and snooping on my phone. But my dad was a different story. I had always been a Daddy's girl. I wished that he'd yelled at me, grounded me, even took my phone for a month. Nope. He just looked at me differently, even treated me differently for a while. I felt like I let him down. Of course, I wasn't trying to hurt him. He was not exactly on my mind when I was fooling around with T.J., but I knew that it was a shock to him. He had a look that I can't put into words. I'll never forget it. It felt like things had changed between us forever.

The thing is I like T.J. and he's super cute but I can't say that I love him. I never thought about that before, but I don't know if I do so. I guess I don't. I didn't think it was fair to him to bring him around my family anymore. He's not a bad guy at all, but I'm sure my dad hates him. How could I have T.J. over my house when my Dad knew what we did? My dad sometimes has trouble looking at me when we speak. My dad would deny that but I feel it. I know kids who have sex with their boyfriend or girlfriend but their parents don't usually know about it. I had no choice. I had to break up with T.J. I could not continue to pour salt on my dad's wounds. I knew that things wouldn't always be this awkward between my dad and me; he would get over this eventually, but for now it was definitely awkward and strained and I didn't think I loved T.J.

For me, the bottom line is I'm just not ready for all this anxiety, stress, and drama. I don't want more pressure or distractions in my life than I already have as a teenager. I want to make my own decisions and not be pressured by my peers or my boyfriend. Isn't that what it means to be a modern woman? I can make my own choices, even if they are unconventional. It shouldn't make me a prude or uncool. That is my decision—I'm just not ready to have sex at 17. Even if everyone else was doing it (which they're not), I'm not ready for this yet.

My life was easier and much less complicated before we had unplanned sex that night. I wonder how often teens have sex because it just goes too far. I never thought about that before. I thought it was always planned. I don't get to hit a delete button and go back no matter how much I want to, but that doesn't mean I have to continue to have sex just because I'm not a virgin. For me this is what it means to be mature and independent. I can make my own decisions and my decision is not to have sex for a while longer and that is ok.

Madelyn: Not Me!!

I don't know why I thought I could never get an STD. I know that they are out there and that people get them from sex. I have been told this not only in school but also by my parents. I have been educated on the risks, the prevalence, and the mode of transmission. I was about 99% positive that I would never get one. I thought that those things happen to other people, not me. I am 20 years old and have only had two sexual partners. I know it only takes one partner, one time. I know that; I've been told. I could not have been more shocked or surprised when I received my diagnosis.

I've thought quite a bit about why I listened but never <u>heard</u> what I was being told. There <u>is</u> a difference. After months of sleepless nights and deep reflection, I still don't have an answer. I have been noticing on the news stories of teenagers or 20-year-olds taking risks and doing very stupid things, sometimes even deadly things like jumping into a hotel pool at a party from the roof of the hotel, or doing 21 shots on your 21st birthday. Both of these stories I saw on the news ended in the tragic death of the teens. I'm sure they were also told that their actions could have dangerous consequences. Those teenagers on the news, they are somewhat like me; they did it anyway probably because they felt invincible. How many of them thought what I foolishly thought? "Those things don't happen to people like me."

Here's what I've been seeing in the news.

Four guys in their early 20s were driving home after drinking all night. At 5 AM, they crashed their car after traveling over a mile in the wrong direction on a major highway. Two passengers are dead and the driver and another buddy are still in critical condition after a week. We all know that drinking and driving is deadly—they knew (they were cops) but they probably thought that bad things only happen to other people.

A fraternity party at a local college just lost its charter today after one student died in a local hospital from alcohol poisoning. She was only 18, probably a freshman. I'm sure she knew that drinking too much can be deadly. I'm also sure she didn't think for one second she would die that night.

Another local young woman that left a club by herself is now missing. There is video footage from the street of some older guy following her. She has been missing for weeks. I bet her parents told her never to go out alone at night—my parents told me this 1000 times—but she did.

I am studying psychology in college. I would love to be able to figure me out, figure us (kids/teens) out, and figure out how to get through to us. I was told all the right things. My parents were involved and talked to my siblings and me **repeatedly** about the dangers of the world outside of our comfortable suburban home. Sometimes it felt like every family dinner was a lecture! In my home growing up, family dinner was sacred. It didn't matter if we ate at 6 PM or 8 PM, if the meal lasted 30 minutes or 5. My parents and my brothers had dinner together almost every single night. My dad read that kids are much less likely to smoke and do drugs if there is a family meal. It shows the parents are interested their children's daily activities and life. We discussed politics, world events, school activities, friends, religion, and all the things parents warn their kids about. I would never do drugs or smoke, but I did have sex. I was still stupidly surprised when I got an STD. I genuinely thought it that only happened to bad people. I know, it's very dumb of me.

The two guys I have been with were clean cut, came from nice families, took care of their health, never smoked, and definitely did not have any bumps or marks on their genitals when I slept with them. One of these clean-cut guys gave me genital warts. I still don't know which one it was. I always used a condom AND spermicide. I was extra careful, was not promiscuous, and always stayed away from the "players" and it still happened to me.

Maybe scientists will find some part of the brain that develops later in life that connects actions to consequences. I have read that our brains don't fully form until around age 25, particularly in boys. That is a very scary thought, but it explains a lot. That can't explain everything, however, because older people do stupid things too. My friend's dad just had an affair and the other woman posted pictures of them together on Facebook. They are in there 40s. Now her parents are getting divorced. The other woman was married too. I guess everyone can make stupid decisions.

So I had a lot of pain and burning. I had to check myself out—yep, I had what looked like pimples on my vagina. I immediately went to see my OB/GYN, Dr. Thompson. She said that I had genital warts, which are caused by the HPV virus. She said I was lucky (I really didn't feel lucky) because the type of HPV I contracted only caused warts. Some of the other strains of HPV can cause cervical cancer (and penile cancer too, so you guys are not safe either). She gave me a prescription for something to make the warts go away. They did go away for a few months, but they kept coming back. I found out that treating the warts only makes the warts go away; it does not treat the virus that causes the warts, HPV. There is no cure for HPV. It has to clear the body on its own but sometimes it just doesn't or it can take a really long time.

It's really embarrassing to be itching down there all the time while I'm sitting in class, out on a date, in a restaurant, or anywhere. It was also painful at times, not to mention distracting. Those warts would not stay away, so finally Dr. T decided to try a different treatment. She decided to treat them using a procedure called electro cauterization. This is where the doctor BURNS the wart off of me using a metal probe heated by an electric current. Yes this is the procedure for those of us "lucky" enough to get the strain that can't actually cause cancer and potentially kill you.

I agreed to write my story for Dr. Thompson because I realized that I did listen to my parents and my teachers only sometimes. I never put a cigarette in my mouth, I never had a one-night stand, never got behind the wheel of a car drunk, never put myself at risk by being drunk and alone at a party. My girlfriends and I always had each other's backs. I guess we listened selectively because we are still immature enough or dumb enough to think we are invincible.

I guess I'm hoping that if teenagers hear these stories from other teenagers, they will realize it does happen to the good kids, the smart kids, the kids that are just like themselves. Listen to me, girls; I know that many of us walk that fine line between wanting to have some fun and not screwing up our lives completely. I'm just telling you sometimes you may not get a second chance. It sucks but you just can't make one mistake sometimes. Those drunk drivers and that girl in the bar won't get a second chance. Look at all those statistics at the end of this book. I believe that a majority of those people, if not all, never thought it would happen to them. It happened to me, and it can happen to you too.

I have one last anecdote to share in this book in case any guys happen to read it. Women basically know that boys will say just about anything to get us in bed. Women are just not like that, so you guys really don't have to worry about us lying. For all of you guys out there who think your girlfriend is going to tell you, listen up. One of my roommates in college got herpes from the first guy she slept with. She went to the student health clinic on campus to get diagnosed. I'm sure that they told Ali all about her disease, transmission, treatment, etc. She didn't seem to believe or maybe comprehend what they told her. She's not stupid; she was probably just in denial.

Anyway, she has told me repeatedly that she has no symptoms and hasn't for well over a year. She only had the symptoms the one time. She's convinced herself that she is not contagious and therefore doesn't have to tell the guys she's with about her STD <u>like she should</u>. She is the nicest, sweetest girl you could meet. She doesn't sleep around at all. It's just that she can't bring herself to discuss her sexual history with the guys she dates (and who could blame her?). Guys, if you would think you are not at risk with a girl like Ali, you'd be surprised **and you'd be wrong**. I know she doesn't do it to be cruel or deceitful. I just think she doesn't want to learn or remember what she was told about her disease because that would mean she'd have to accept it herself that she has a lifelong diagnosis and she'd have to tell any or every future boyfriend. Like I said, I believe she's in deep denial. Boys, don't assume you are safe; you just can't know no matter what you think.

Julianna: Super G

Her first serious boyfriend, Patrick, dumped my best friend, Addison. I was actually happy about the breakup even though she was really upset. I never liked the guy. I thought she could do much better. He wasn't all that smart and when he was with his friends, he acted like a real barbarian. Addy was so happy to be in a somewhat serious relationship. I think she overlooked quite a few of Patrick's shortcomings. She was really sad, even somewhat depressed, I would say, after the breakup. I was kind of surprised she took it so badly. Addy is pretty, smart, ambitious, and really an overall great girl. She is also shy and very conservative. She is a very serious person who often doesn't know how to have a good time. I think she struggles with her self-esteem because she doesn't get a lot of attention from guys. She's very pretty but she doesn't really flirt or dress to show her assets, which I respect, but as a result she rarely gets attention from guys. She also has suffered from an episode of depression after her parents' divorce.

As Addy's best friend, I felt a duty to get her out of her funk and perpetual bad mood. I firmly believe that the quickest way to get over a guy is to meet a new guy! I was determined to get her over this dumb boy and not waste any more tears over him. When the weekend came, I knew what I had to do. We were going out to the hottest new club in the city for a girls' night out. I was going to convince Addy how much fun two single girls can have. I was single at the time (a rarity for me). We were going to have so much fun. We have never both been single at the same time before. It was going to be great! I just had to get my friend back out there.

I picked Addy up Friday night ready for a night of drinking and dancing. She tried her best to convince me to stay in and watch movies that night but I was not losing that battle. When we got to the club, I immediately noticed some cute guys checking us out. Addy was still depressed and had a "don't even try to talk to me" look on her face. You know they call it resting bitch face now. I ordered drinks and shots for us. The only way to make this night a success was to get some drinks into my girl. I had to loosen her up. She was going to forget all about what's his name by the end of the night.

I'm not much of a drinker. I absolutely hate everything about a hangover, but I kept thinking about my goal for the night and that was to help my friend. I kept ordering shots. I got really drunk that night. I was so focused on cheering up my friend that I was not paying attention to what was happening to me. I was so drunk that I don't remember most of what happened that night. The thing is I RARELY get drunk. I just like to get buzzed. After my last bad hangover, I decided there is no reason to get wasted, just a little tipsy. You know, it's easier to talk to guys and dance if you have a little buzz.

Addy must have been dumping her shots without me noticing or she can really hold her liquor because she was totally fine. Thank God because at the end of the night, she saved me instead of me trying to save her. You probably noticed that the name of this chapter is not Addison; it's Julianna—that's me. The next day I started to remember some of the horrific details of that night.

At some point during that night, Addy and I got separated. I don't remember how we always, always stayed together in a club. My Dad always warned me since I was a kid to "use the buddy system." He must have told my sister and me that 1000 times. It was good advice and I always listened to him until that night. Anyway, God, this is really hard to tell. I remember a group of guys talking about a bet involving blowjobs, and I vaguely remember me in a very drunken stupor briefly doing just that somewhere in the club, very, very briefly, you know just to win the bet. You may or may not believe me, and I understand and accept that but this behavior is completely not in my character at all. I still can't believe I got drunk enough to do what I did, even as a bet or a joke, even for a few seconds. I don't even know where in the club I was or who these guys were. Addy finally found me passed out in a bathroom stall. She dragged me out to the car and drove us home. She literally carried me home, I don't know how; I have 25, ok 30 pounds on her.

I was so stupid that night. I think about how much worse it could have been. I could have been raped. I'm so extremely disappointed in myself for putting myself at risk like I did. My dad also always said, "The road to Hell is paved with good intentions." I never really knew what he meant until that night. God, does he have to be right about that too? I honestly would never, ever have sex with a stranger, in a club. That's just not me. It's not how I was raised. Girls, here is my warning—know your limits with alcohol. I had no idea what I was doing and it is a very scary place to be in. I don't have any idea how many drinks I had that night. I've never done anything like that in my life and wouldn't have believed you if you said I would have, but I did.

After a two-day hangover, I went to see my OB/GYN, Dr. T, to get checked for STDs. A few years ago, I got a cold sore on my bottom lip that kept coming back. My sister told me it was herpes. I didn't believe her so I made an appointment with someone who would know. I saw Dr. Thompson. She said yes it is a form of herpes. It never really goes away. It goes away and then comes back weeks, months, even years later. Dr. T explained to me that years ago HSV (Herpes Simplex Virus) Type I was typically above the waist and Type II was below the waist. Today with oral sex being more common now Herpes Type I and II can be both above and below the waist. She told me it is contagious and I can give it to someone when kissing or giving oral sex. I basically can give a partner genital herpes with my cold sore. I really hope that guy that took advantage of my drunkenness at the club has genital herpes. I know that is wrong to wish that but what he did was worse.

Anyway, back to present day. In Dr. T's waiting room, I saw a brochure about gonorrhea right in front of me. I was paranoid; I mean I just had oral sex with a total stranger even though I think it was only for a few seconds. It could have been longer, my memory is not clear still, but as far as contracting a disease, it doesn't matter if it was 5 seconds or 5 minutes. I had a feeling right then and there I had gonorrhea. When I went into the patient room, there on the wall was a poster about, you guessed it, gonorrhea. I knew it had to be a sign. I was being punished for my bad behavior. Well, I can't really say punished; I made a very bad decision and now I'll have to face the consequences. I knew all about herpes but nothing really about gonorrhea, so I got my iPhone out and started searching about what I was in for. After a 10-minute search I was literally sweating bullets. I found out that…

- Fellatio is the most efficient way to spread gonorrhea.
- My state has a much higher incidence of gonorrhea than most others.
- There is something called SUPER GONORRHEA. Yep. I call it SUPER G. It's resistant to almost all of the drugs that used to be used to treat this disease.
- In 2013 and 2014, the number of resistant gonorrhea strains doubled.
- The number of cases of gonorrhea were at historic lows in 2009 but have increased every year since then.
- Most US cases of gonorrhea are among adolescents and young adults.
- Untreated gonorrhea can cause infertility and sterility.

I thought I was pretty informed because I knew all about herpes and how it spread. I never heard of Super Gonorrhea before and I pay attention to the news quite a bit, unlike most of my friends. I read the book in Dr. T's waiting room last time I was here. I can't believe resistant gonorrhea is such a problem and I never heard about it. The problem has never come across any of my social media feeds. Girls, here's some more advice. Oral sex is not safe sex or even safer sex. You can't get pregnant but you can still get a pretty nasty STD with long-term consequences, and let's face it, no one uses condoms for oral sex. I also learned from Veronica in Dr. T's book that condom isn't always the answer. They don't work as well for STDs transmitted through skin-on-skin contact. I can't believe gonorrhea is easier to spread from oral sex than actual intercourse. Who knew? Certainly not me or any of my friends.

My mom told me that the smartest people she knows are not the ones with the highest IQ, the most degrees, or the best paying jobs. The smartest people are ones who learn from their mistakes. Well that makes me a genius. I'll never lose control from alcohol ever again. See, Mom and Dad, I do listen and I definitely learned from my mistakes. Hopefully whoever reads this story, more accurately this nightmare, can learn from my mistake and avoid getting an STD or worse. Thankfully I didn't have gonorrhea or anything else. I dodged a bullet that night, literally. Gonorrhea can be serious. I can't even imagine having an STD especially from some unknown, random guy or being raped that night. I can't even think about that.

One more thing. Everyone I know my age, every age actually, even my grandmother, has an iPhone and therefore Internet access anytime, anywhere. Kids my age grew up using the Internet, Chromebooks, smart-phones, Kindles, etc. We can access more information faster than any generation before us. My parents told me they had to go to the library for their research papers when they were in school. We literally have every bit of information at our fingertips 24/7. So next time you have a 10-minute wait for the bus or to pick up your little brother at soccer practice, do yourself a favor; skip Instagram and search an STD, any STD for 10 minutes. You'll be amazed (and not in a good way) at what you can find out. EDUCATE YOURSELF.

STDs are on the rise in spite the use of new vaccines and years of promotion of condoms and safe sex. Arm yourself with knowledge, protect your bodies, don't get too drunk, be smart, and don't be asked to write your own chapter. Learn from my mistakes. That will make you even smarter than me.

Dr. Melanie Thompson:
Cleared for Take Off

I am a physician and a mom. I have been in private practice for 23 years and a mom for 17 years. I see approximately 100 patients a week in my office, all women. The primary reason I got into gynecology and obstetrics is because I could not think of a better career than helping bring beautiful new babies safely into this world. I have delivered hundreds of infants but it never, ever loses its excitement for me. I don't mind getting that phone call at 3 AM to report to the hospital. It's the best job in the world. Delivering babies is why I went into obstetrics. I almost feel like a superhero because I know I play a role in bringing another healthy soul to earth. I still get excited when meeting new parents for the first time. But something else has fueled my passion after over two decades of treating women.

My heart, my mission is now not only wrapped up in my pregnant ladies; it is also now equally consumed with sexual health. I never envisioned in my early days as a resident that the **GIFT** of seeing a patient before she become sexually active would be as rewarding as delivering a newborn baby. I never considered the unfortunate timing of seeing young girls **after** they became sexually active would prove to be so frustrating. When I see young women before they have sex for the first time, I get the opportunity, the reward, of discussing the risks and complications of sex with them. I get a **chance** to educate them, to give them a glimpse of what I have seen in over 20 years of practice. I get to share with them the grim facts about diseases, contraception, pregnancy, and infertility. When I get that chance to enlighten someone so they can **make more informed decisions**, I feel fulfilled and accomplished. It's not my job to talk people out of having sex. It is my job, however, to make sure they understand and to know the facts before making their decision.

When my son was about 10 years old, he was mildly obsessed with superheroes. We had seen a plethora of the latest superhero movies: Thor, Iron Man, Captain America, Batman, Superman, etc. My son and I had several conversations about which superhero had the best superpower. He asked me repeatedly, "Mom, if you could pick one superpower to have, what would it be?" This was a topic of discussion between us for weeks, maybe even months. How does a 10-year-old boy choose between flying, X-ray vision, running at the speed of sound, or being able to scale buildings with spider webbing? At first I just picked something, anything to engage the conversation. After having the same conversation over and over, I admit I began to actually think about it.

I decided it would be really cool if I could make myself invisible. I'd love to be able to go behind the scenes at the Oscars or spy on my teenager at a party. That would be awesome. I soon realized that very little good, if any, would come from that but what if I had the power to make other people invisible. I could have teenage girls shadow me for the day. If you could see what I see and hear what I hear, I predict you would wait a bit longer and not rush into having sex. It's one thing to read these stories, and hopefully they have made an impact on you; it's quite another to see the crying, the physical pain, rashes, depression, infertility, lesions, bugs (yes, crabs and scabies are bugs), broken hearts, anxiety, and open sores over and over again, day in and day out. By the way, there are even more STDs than the ones mentioned in this book. I have also seen patients with scabies, chancroid (an extremely painful condition), trichomoniasis (a common disease which can also cause Pelvic Inflammatory Disease and premature babies), candida (look that one up, it's really terrible), Hepatitis B, and Hepatitis A (which both can cause severe liver problems), just to name a few.

When I flew to Atlanta for a medical conference last week, I sat at the airport waiting area looking out of those large floor-to-ceiling windows at all those airplanes. Each one gets checked, cleaned, gassed up, and prepared for takeoff. I wish I could somehow make sure all girls (and boys) got "cleared for takeoff." I wish very single young adult had to first talk to me, or someone like me. I would discuss the risks, how to reduce the risks, the consequences, the diseases, the emotional struggles, the complications that can happen from having sex, particularly at a young age. I would also discuss how special sex can be under the right circumstances. Teens all need to have that conversation and be "cleared for takeoff." They need to understand the possible outcomes before engaging in sexual activity **of any kind**. Unfortunately too many of our young people are going in blind, unaware of many of the consequences that accompany sexual activity. Many think that simply using condoms will ensure their safety. Some of my patients have a good awareness of diseases but still believe, foolishly, that these diseases are rare so it will not happen to them. Trust me, STDs are not rare at all. My mission is to tell the truth, warts and all, because forever is a really long time.

In Case You Missed It

1. Nearly **20 million new** sexually transmitted diseases occur every year in this country, half among young people in the ages of 15–24.

2. Most individuals with HSV-1 or HSV-2 are asymptomatic or have very mild symptoms. As a result, 87.4% of infected individuals remain unaware of their infection

3. HSV-2 infection is **more common among women** than among men (20.3% vs. 10.6%). Infection is more easily transmitted from men to women than from women to men.

4. As the result of undiagnosed STDs, like chlamydia and gonorrhea, every year **24,000** American women become infertile.

5. Anyone who is sexually active can get HPV, even if you have had sex with only one partner.

6. You can get HPV by having vaginal, anal, or oral sex with someone who has the virus.

7. HPV is the most common STI. HPV is so common that over half of all sexually active men and women get it at some point in their lives.

8. HPV can cause cervical and other common cancers including cancer of the vulva, vagina, penis, or anus. It can also cause cancer in throat, including the base of the tongue and tonsils. Cancer often takes years, even decades to develop after a person gets HPV.

9. More than 10,000 women in the United States get cervical cancer each year.

10. There is no way to know which people who have the HPV virus will develop cancer or other health problems.

11. Most people with untreated syphilis do not develop late-stage syphilis. However, when it does happen, it is very serious and can occur 10–30 years after your infection began. Symptoms of late syphilis include paralysis, numbness, blindness, and dementia.

12. One in four sexually active adolescent females have an STD.

13. Young women's bodies are biologically more susceptible to STDs than men's.

14. Genital ulcerative disease caused by herpes makes it easier to acquire HIV infection sexually. There is an estimated 2- to 4-fold increased risk of acquiring HIV when genital herpes is present. This is because genital herpes can cause ulcers or breaks in the skin or mucous membranes (lining of the mouth, vagina, and rectum) which compromises the protection normally provided by the skin and mucous membranes.

15. In 2012, 1,002,692 cases of chlamydia infection were reported among persons under 25 years of age, representing 70% of all reported chlamydia cases.

16. Protection against genital ulcer diseases and HPV depends on the site of the sore/ulcer or infection. Latex condoms can only protect against transmission when the ulcers or infections are in genital areas that are covered or protected by the condom.

17. When someone has a cold sore on their mouth or simply an oral infection with no sores present, and is the giver of oral sex to someone else, the virus can spread from the mouth of the infected person to the genitals of the uninfected person. The receiver of the oral sex might then get genital herpes.

18. Many people who get herpes outbreaks around the rectum and the buttocks have never had anal sex. This can occur when the virus travels along a slightly different nerve pathway to get to the surface of the skin than the one that innervates the genitals.

19. Men can have the virus present (HSV) inside of the urethra with no external sores. Virus can be given off from the genital skin of both men and women with no sores, through microscopic breaks in the skin.

20. Up to 70% of new cases of herpes are transmitted from some-one showing no apparent symptoms at the time they infect their partner.

Estimated Number of **NEW** STIs in the United States, 2008

Hepatitis B	19,000
HIV	41,000
Syphilis	54,400
HSV	2,776,000
Gonorrhea	820,000
Trichomoniasis	1,090,000
Chlamydia	2,860,000
HPV	14,100,000

*One in five Americans currently has an STD (most thought it would never happen to them).

Addendum

Our own patient and contributor to the journal, McKenzie, has moved on to California and endeavored in a very successful film career. We at Tri County OB/GYN could not be prouder of her and all the brave contributors to our humbly initiated booklet. Here is an update from this very talented, passionate, ambitious, and gifted young lady. I also want to personally thank these women who were willing to rehash and retell their experiences and write them down in an effort to educate others. Here is proof that one person can make a difference in this world.

—Dr. Evelyn Thompson

I landed at LAX on a Thursday evening. My vision of my future life in Los Angeles starts with a perfect sunny day, beach weather, and beautiful, fashionable, fit people everywhere. I fantasized about my voice, my view, my vision being parlayed into a blockbuster movie or critically acclaimed TV documentary at the very least. Perhaps my own weekly column in a trendy fashion or political magazine would be in my future. Funny thing about dreams, people tend to dream about the success part, not about all the work, effort, sweat, tears, and failure before arriving. It was raining and foggy when the plane landed that Thursday afternoon in June, perhaps a sign that the days of blissful sunshine and success I fully expected and planned would be at times spoiled by gray skies and puddles.

I was pragmatic enough to plan on starting at the bottom and eventually ascending all the way to the top of Hollywood, to one day be writing and producing my projects and my ideas, spreading my dogma from the top of my proverbial lungs. However, after year of toiling at the bottom, I only ascended to the lower middle, not a place of power and not a place to run wild with my creativity. I read profusely in my free time. Funny thing, I was just not that interested in dating at that moment in my life. Maybe it's my past history with men, maybe it was just my time to focus on my career. I was half way through reading a book on execution (of ideas) when I realized that there was nothing stopping me from executing my own project, or at the very least starting one. I decided to begin and see where the creative journey would take me.

I wrote down all my ideas, pages of ideas, and quickly scratched off almost all of them after careful review. I chiseled my list down to my top five. One problem was echoing in my head, and I could not shake it off. Not one of my ideas was comparable in quality, originality, importance, and messaging to something reverberating from my past. You guessed it. As I mentioned before, I read quite a bit since I arrived in LA. I just finished reading another book titled *Steal Like an Artist*. Generally speaking, the stealing is more akin to finding and using a muse. We all need inspiration beyond the beautiful west coast landscapes. THE JOURNAL.

Dr. Thompson's folio was exactly the type of communiqué I wanted to put out into the universe: informative, educational, and filling a gap of knowledge. It was perfect in content, realism, originality, and relevance to today's world. So what if it wasn't 100% my original idea! I'm comfortable with sharing credit!

When you see "I Wish I Knew" in a theatre or bookstore near you, you will know the back story of how the artist, me, saw a first-rate idea and turned it into something for even more women to see, hear, feel, experience, and learn from. All I had to do was accept that I had the power. I could either wait for someone to ask me for my ideas or I could initiate them on my own ambition. It was my idea to render the concept and to see the final product **executed**. I love that word—execute. Sincere admiration and eternal gratitude to Dr. T who is the true genesis of a brilliant, life-altering, life-saving idea.

Works Cited

Centers for Disease Control and Prevention. Centers for Disease Control
  and Prevention, 06 Jan. 2015. Web. 11 Feb. 2015.

"Heritage House '76, Pro-Life Supplies for the Pro-Life Movement."
  Heritage House '76, Pro-Life Supplies for the Pro-Life Movement. N.p.,
  n.d. Web. 05 Mar. 2015.

HPV/Oral Cancer Facts. Oral Cancer Foundation.org. 01 Feb. 2019. The
  Oral Cancer Foundation. 15 May 2019. Oralcancerfoundation.org

Love, Shayla. *Why It Matters if HPV Caused Your Head or Neck Cancer.*
  Vice.com. 12 Jan. 2018. 15 May 2019

Marie McCullough, *HPV Is Causing an Oral cancer Epidemic in Men
  by Outwitting Natural Defenses.* The Philadelphia Inquirer. 12 Mar.
  2018. 15 May 2019. ChicagoTribune.com

Warren, Terri Gunn, and Ricks Warren. *The Updated Herpes Handbook.*
  Portland, OR: Portland, 1985. Print.